Call Me Charlotte

Dana L. Brown

Book 2 in the AMI Series

Published by:
Southern Yellow Pine (SYP) Publishing
4351 Natural Bridge Rd.
Tallahassee, FL 32305

www.syppublishing.com

This is a work of fiction. Names, characters, places, and events that occur either are the products of the author's imagination or are used fictitiously. Any resemblance to actual persons, places, or events is purely coincidental.

The contents and opinions expressed in this book do not necessarily reflect the views and opinions of Southern Yellow Pine Publishing, nor does the mention of brands or trade names constitute endorsement.

ISBN-13: 978-1-59616-068-2
ISBN-13: ePub 978-1-59616-069-9
ISBN-13: Adobe PDF eBook 978-1-59616-071-2
Library of Congress Control Number: 2018941831

Printed in the United States of America
First Edition
April 2018

Dedication

This book is dedicated to all the people who loved *Lottie Loser* and said they couldn't wait for *Call Me Charlotte* to be released! Thank you! Without you my Fairytale would be just a faraway dream.

Plus, a huge Thank You to my friend, Nancy Waltz, for her continual support and encouragement. No one worked harder or cared more than she did.

And last to my family, who was always there for support and encouragement. I love you.

Prologue

I had never felt so much quiet while being surrounded by so much noise. The sirens were blaring and communications were coming in over the scanner, but squeezed between Noah and Pop, the three of us holding hands, all I could hear were my own thoughts, and they weren't pretty.

"My name is Charlotte Luce, and I'm the youngest, and first female market president in the history of Olde Florida Bank. Well, I was before they fired me. The bank called it an amicable split, but let's be honest, I was fired. I loved my job with Olde Florida, and I was good at it, but a difference of opinion, about my decision to support my assistant after she and her brother were arrested, caused a big stink, so now I'm unemployed.

My gran used to say things happen for a reason, and I think she was right. There's no way I could be thinking about banking right now because there's a man lying in the hospital, possibly fighting for his life, and there's something he needs to know. I never stopped loving him either."

Chapter 1

Now

Noah seemed unable to move so Charlotte put her arms around him and asked the question that was turning her stomach inside out. "He's okay though, right Noah? Nick's going to be okay?"

Noah snapped out of his trance, squeezed her tight, and stepped back. "I don't know, Lottie," he said hoarsely. "Nick's boss called Pop and told him he was sending a sheriff's deputy to pick him up because he needs to get there fast. I've got to get home before the deputy gets there." He started for the door and looked back at her. "Well aren't you coming?"

They wanted her to come? Surely, they knew about the fight she and Nick had, maybe even the awful things she had said. But at that moment, Charlotte didn't care, she needed to be with Nick, and Noah was giving her a lifeline. Nodding her head, she grabbed Noah's hand and let him lead her into the still Florida morning.

The deputy from the Anna Maria Island Sheriff's department was just pulling up when Noah and Charlotte arrived. Pop's eyes were red from crying, but he still gave her a weak smile and a hug. "I'm so glad you came, Lottie," he said, choking back his tears. "Nick would want you here and so do Noah and I."

The three of them crammed in the back of the squad car and held on to each other for dear life. *Nick's young and strong*, Charlotte thought. *He'll be okay, right? He has to be okay.* She wanted to reach up and touch her locket from Gran, but she didn't dare let go of Noah and Pop's hands. Instead she closed her eyes and talked to her beloved Grandmother through her thoughts, just as she always did when she needed comfort. It helped a little, but when she opened her eyes she saw the way Nick's face had looked when she sent him away, and nothing could stop her mind from reliving the whole awful fight.

It was the evening the news had broken that Carol Neel, Charlotte's Administrative Assistant, and her brother Tony had been arrested on racketeering charges by the FBI. And not by just any FBI Agent, but her FBI Agent, the man had been her childhood friend and the love of her life since she was nine years old. Charlotte had been devastated when the bank's CEO, Martin Riggs, had shared the news with her, and her sense of betrayal and outrage came to the surface when Nick came to explain.

Nick had done his best to get her to listen to what he had to say, but Charlotte had stood firm on her anger. She wouldn't let him touch her when he tried, and when he said, "You have to know I never meant any of this to hurt you," and then, "This was strictly business," she had lost it.

But it was the words he said after that haunted her. "I love you Charlotte. I've never stopped loving you, and if you will just let me explain from the beginning, I know you will understand."

She wouldn't listen however, and instead taunted him with memories of the other man who had loved her, the man she given her virginity to, the beautiful man who had wanted to marry her and share a life with her. "But I couldn't", she had spat at him, "because deep down I hoped by some miracle we'd find each other someday, and I ended up breaking Ryan's heart."

Just before she had shown him out the door, Nick had tried once more to appeal to her heart by saying, "Don't run out on us again, Lottie," and it was then she had thrown the final blow.

"There is no us, Nick," she had hissed at him, "I don't think there ever was. Just a girl looking for a fairytale, and a guy wanting to get in her pants."

Chapter 2

Now

The ride to Tampa General seemed to go on forever, but when they arrived, Charlotte was amazed to see that the normal one-hour drive only took around thirty minutes. The deputy dropped them off at the Emergency Room entrance, and the Deputy Director of the Tampa FBI Field Office was there to meet them. Charlotte hung back, knowing it was Pop the director was waiting for, so why did she feel like if looks could kill, she'd be dead?

"Mr. Greyson, I'm David James, with the FBI Field office," he said, reaching out to shake Pop's hand. "I know you want answers about how Nick is doing, but right now, I just don't have them. I won't lie to you though, he's in bad shape, but the best thoracic surgeon in the state is working on him right now, and I imagine it will be several hours before we hear anything."

Pop and Noah both paled even more than before and Charlotte did her best not to come unglued. *They need me now*, she said to herself and reached over to touch Pop's shoulder. Noah spoke first.

"What happened?" he asked. "The last I heard Nick was spending a lot of time on desk duty, not out in the field."

Director James wiped his hand over his face before answering. "I don't have the answer for that either," he stated. "Nick was working on a lot of paperwork and not taking new cases while he worked through some things, but the shooting happened at his home. It appears he was shot in the chest at close range and then tried to go down the stairs after his assailant. The best we can put together is he became weak from blood loss and fell the rest of the way down, which was about two flights. A neighbor found him in the foyer unconscious when she returned home from a late night and called 911." He stopped for a moment to let it sink in and added, "So now we're dealing with a gunshot wound as well as a severe head trauma."

Charlotte had never been so afraid. Her whole world was laying on an operating table someplace inside that hospital, and she was powerless to do anything. Except talk to Gran, of course. She reached up, touched her locket and prayed that somehow, she would have the strength and the courage to help Nick's family through this, and that she would be given a second, no third chance, to make things right between them.

Charlotte heard Pop tell the director that he needed to call Nick's mom and sister, just as Noah spoke up. "Why don't you call Maya, Pop," Noah said, "and I'll call Mom?" Pop nodded his approval and both men stepped away to make the calls. Leaving Charlotte alone with Deputy Director James.

"I take it you're Ms. Luce," he said to her in a harsh and condescending manner.

"Ye…Yes, but how do you know my name?" she stammered.

"Well let me see. First, Agent Greyson asked to be taken off a case he's been working on for over a year, because he felt it was a conflict of interest, you know given your *friendship*." The way he emphasized friendship made Charlotte cringe, but she held her tongue. "And then you threw a fit when two people who are threatening the security of our nation were arrested. But mostly it's from finding out you hired Owen Gardner to represent Carol Neel, and then finding out from Martin Riggs that you work for Olde Florida Bank and were told specifically to stay out of the investigation. I know all about you Miss Luce, and I don't like any of it."

Charlotte squared her shoulders and stood up to her full five foot ten-inch height, which put her looking directly into the eyes of the Field Director. "First, Deputy Director," she said, copying his style, "my friendship with Nick Greyson isn't really any of your business. If he chose to share it with you, that was his call, but I won't. And second, the FBI used my friendship with Nick to get information on Carol Neel, and I find that reprehensible. Legal? Maybe, but wrong just the same.

And last, yes, I did hire Owen Gardner, and I'd do it again in a heartbeat. You and I both know that Carol is just a pawn in your case against her brother, and it makes me both angry and appalled at the same time. You don't have to like me Director James, but until Nick tells me to leave, we may be seeing a lot of each other."

Director James looked at Charlotte and told her honestly. "No wonder Agent Greyson has been all tied up in knots," and walking away, he chuckled under his breath. "Charlotte Luce is both gutsy and gorgeous!"

Chapter 3

Now

"Maya and Dimi are on their way from Tarpon Springs," Pop told them when he returned, "How did it go with your Mother, Noah?"

"Mom and Gus are on a River Cruise through France right now, and not really in a good position to leave. I'm supposed to keep her updated and let her know if there's a change in Nick's condition."

Charlotte felt as if her heart had been ripped out when she heard Pop swear. She knew that he and his ex-wife had issues, but obviously he thought she would want to be at Nick's side. "Everyone who matters will be here when Nick gets out of surgery," he said, as if trying to convince himself, "and that's what makes our family so strong."

Noah put his arm around his Dad, and Charlotte joined in for a group hug, feeling both blessed and unworthy to be considered a part of the Greyson family.

Knowing it was going to be a long day, the four of them settled in the surgery wing waiting room. "I need to call Becca and Jared," Charlotte said before sitting down. "Jared is a doctor in New Smyrna, and he might be able to help in some way. Can I bring anyone coffee when I come back?"

All three men accepted her offer, and Charlotte went back outside so she could use her cell. As soon as Becca answered, the tears Charlotte had been holding back came out with a fury, and it wasn't until she calmed down that Becca could even understand her.

"Nick's been shot, and he fell down two flights of stairs, and he's in surgery; what if I don't ever get the chance to tell him I love him?"

"Take a deep breath," her friend coached her, "and try to calm down. Jared just ran to the office, but he has the weekend off, so as soon as I can get the kids squared away, we'll head to Tampa. I'll be saying my Rosary, and I'll get everyone in our prayer chain doing theirs, too."

Just talking with Becca gave Charlotte some peace. "You guys don't have to come all this way," she told her friend. "Just being able to talk with you has helped."

"Nonsense, Lottie Lou," Becca scolded. "You are my sister in every way but by birth, and Jared and I belong there with you. Now, is there anything you need?"

"Well," Charlotte replied meekly. "We had to take off quickly so I'm dressed in shorts and a T-shirt. I'd love to at least have a pair of jeans and a sweatshirt, and maybe some undies? I'm not sure when I'll make it home."

Becca laughed. "You got it, Sweetie. I'll let you know when we get close so you can tell me where to meet you. Stay strong Lottie, the Greyson guys need you now, just as much as you need them. See you soon."

Charlotte hung up feeling as if a weight had been lifted off her heart. She got directions to the cafeteria and headed for some much-needed caffeine.

Chapter 4

Now

Settled back in the waiting room with Pop, Noah, and Director James, Charlotte closed her eyes and thought back over the events of the past twenty-four hours. She had lost her job; Carol's attorney was optimistic that he would be able to get her released and possibly get the charges against her dropped. Noah had explained how Nick and the FBI had come to get the information about Carol's brother, Tony, and that Nick had been shot. And oh yeah, Noah had pretty much professed his love for her. She had experienced some crazy days in her life, but this one had to top them all.

The hustle and bustle of the busy hospital was somehow soothing after the quiet of the ride from Anna Maria, and before she realized it, Charlotte drifted off to sleep. She dreamt of Nick and memories of the innocent years of their friendship when happiness was swimming in the gulf or sharing sodas from Two Scoops.

"Do you ever see your mom, Nick?" she asked him. "I know your parents are divorced, but there's a picture of her on Pop's desk, and no one ever mentions her name."

"My dad says he's still in love with her," Nick answered, "even though she remarried right after we moved to New York. The main reason we came back to the island is because Mom's new husband wants to travel, and we need to be in school. Pop keeps saying that she'll come to her senses and come back home one day, but she won't. I wish he would forget about her, but I guess love does strange things to a person."

"Kind of like my mom not being able to move on from my dad? If that's what love does to a person, I don't want any part of it."

She remembered that Nick had given her a funny smile and then said, "Come on, let's walk on the beach."

Charlotte woke with a start. How long had she been asleep, and what time was it? She was embarrassed that she had fallen asleep while Pop and Noah were rigidly sitting, waiting for word on Nick. Of course, in the truly gracious style of Nicholas Greyson, Pop just squeezed her hand and said, "I'm so glad you got some rest, Lottie."

Sometime while she was asleep, Maya and Dimitri had arrived and were huddled together on a couch with Noah. Shortly after twelve noon a doctor stepped into the waiting room, asking for the family of Nick Greyson. Nick had been in surgery for hours and the few minutes waiting for an answer seemed to her almost as long.

"I'm Nick's father," Pop said with conviction, "and we are his family." Charlotte thought she heard a cough from Director James when Pop included her as part of Nick's family, but that wasn't important now. Only Nick was.

Reaching out to shake Pop's hand, the doctor introduced herself. "I'm Dr. Suzan Copeland, Mr. Greyson. Your son made it through the surgery, but he's in critical condition. The bullet just missed his heart, but it still did major damage. We've repaired the severed blood vessels and the wound, but the next forty-eight hours are crucial."

"Is he going to make it, Dr. Copeland?" Noah asked, but she wouldn't give him any kind of false hope.

"Agent Greyson is young and healthy, two important things to hold on to. Whenever the brain is involved there's always concern, and right now, I don't have all the answers about his head injury. There's definitely swelling, and a neurosurgeon is evaluating him, but repairing the chest was our first course of action."

"Can we see him?" Pop asked with tears in his eyes. "I need to see my boy."

Dr. Copeland gave him a weak smile. "I understand Mr. Greyson, and as soon as Dr. Rivers is done with his evaluation, I will allow one person in at a time for five minutes, but family only. He's in the Critical Care Unit (CCU), and if everything goes all right overnight, I'll see about different arrangements tomorrow. Any other questions?"

"Thank you, Dr. Copeland," Pop said to her. "Thank you so much for saving my son. Director James said that you're the best surgeon in the state, and I feel confident Nick will pull through."

Chapter 5

Now

Dr. Copeland had just left the waiting room when Becca and Jared walked in. "I thought you were going to call me?" Charlotte questioned.

Putting her arms around her friend, Becca replied, "I didn't realize my husband was so familiar with Tampa General. He knew exactly where you would be so we came on up. Has there been any change?"

Charlotte was just getting ready to tell them about their visit with Dr. Copeland, when Noah cut in. "Sister Rebecca Rose is that you?" he asked, looking down at her very visible baby bump.

Becca slapped him on the shoulder and gave him a big hug. "The Sister part pretty much ended when I met him," she said pointing to her husband, "but the Rebecca Rose is still accurate. Anyway, the island isn't big enough that you missed the news that I got married," she teased him. "My Mom likes to tell people she lost a Nun but gained a Son."

Jared stepped forward and shook hands with Pop, Noah, and Dimitri, and gave a polite nod to Maya. "So, what have you been told?" he asked in all out-doctor mode. "I hope that Suzan Copeland was here for the surgery?"

After sharing what they learned with Jared, he excused himself to see if he could get any more information. Becca was just about to take Charlotte to the lady's room to change when Director James got a phone call. "I see," he said very guardedly, "I'll be right there."

Turning to Pop, and the waiting room filled with Nick's family and friends, he said, "We may have just gotten a break concerning Nick's assailant. A woman in a condo one over from Nick's was trying to get a fussy baby to sleep and saw a man running from his building around three a.m. this morning. When she heard about the shooting, she called the local police station and they called our office. I'm going to meet her as soon as I can get there, and hope that she has some usable information."

The deputy director stopped for a moment and added, "Mr. Greyson, your son is one of the finest agents I've ever had the privilege of working with, and I promise you, we'll get whoever did this to him."

Both Pop and Noah got up and shook his hand, but before he could leave, Charlotte stopped him. "Director James, may I speak with you a moment, please?" she asked. He nodded and motioned for her to step out in the hall with him.

"I want to apologize for the things I said earlier," she said softly. "It's not really like me to be so combative, but it's been a tough couple of weeks, and the last twenty-four hours have been even worse. I'm not sorry for helping Carol, but I am sorry if the things Nick was working through involved me."

Director James smiled for the first time. "I appreciate the apology and to be honest I owe you one as well. We're on the same team, Miss Luce, and we both want a full recovery for Agent Greyson. Martin told me you were special, and now I see why." He started to move on and Charlotte stopped him again.

"Thank you, Director James, and please, call me Charlotte."

Chapter 6

Now

The tension in the waiting room was explosive, and Charlotte hated seeing the stress on Pop's face. She assumed his health was good but knew the only thing that was going to relieve it was to see Nick and to know that he was okay. She was just about ready to go over to him when Jared returned, followed by another doctor.

"Mr. Greyson," Jared said facing Pop. "This is Doctor William Rivers, a good friend of mine and the best neurosurgeon in the state."

Pop shook hands with the doctor and asked again, "How is he?"

"Head injuries aren't always as easy to assess as, say, his gunshot wound. What we do know is he has swelling on his brain but no visible signs of bleeding. I looked at the results of his CT scan right before I came out here, and I'm guardedly optimistic. We are going to keep him in a drug induced coma for the next few days to see if the swelling goes down on its own and to watch for other complications. We have him in CCU with a very skilled nursing team, and they'll let me know immediately if there are any changes. Do you have any questions?"

And once again Pop asked, "When can I see my son?"

Dr. Rivers smiled and said a nurse would be out shortly to take him back, but only for five minutes. He reiterated what Dr. Copeland had said about family only, and one person at a time.

Jared thanked his friend and came back to stand with Becca and Charlotte. "Nick is in the best hands possible," he told them, "but now all we can do is wait and pray."

True to his word a nurse came out about fifteen minutes later and went directly to Pop. "Mr. Greyson," she said, "my name is Shelly Bert, and I'm the Patient Advocate and Family Liaison for the hospital's

Critical Care Unit. I'll be working very closely with both Dr. Copeland and Dr. Rivers, but I'm here for you, so please don't hesitate to talk with me if you have any questions or concerns, Okay? Now how about I take you back to your son? I know how hard the waiting is, but I assure you we are taking great care of him."

Pop looked at the kind face of the nurse and smiled. "Thank you, Mrs. Bert, I appreciate that more than you know."

"It's actually Miss Bert," she responded, "but you're welcome to call me Shelly. I think we're going to be spending a lot of time together." She flashed Pop a genuine smile and led him through the door.

Becca grabbed Charlotte's hand and asked if she was ready to change her clothes. She answered with a nod, leaving Jared alone with Noah, Maya, and Dimitri. "Tell us the truth, Jared," Noah beseeched. "What are my brother's chances of ever walking out of this hospital?"

Jared used his best bed-side manner to answer honestly, without minimizing the seriousness of the situation. "As I said before, you have the two best doctors in the state taking care of Nick, and I would want them on the case if it was my family member involved. The other important element is Nick's will to recover. That may sound simple, but he must want to get better and have a reason to. From what I've seen, he's surrounded by love, and that's a strong motivator."

Noah ran his hands over his face and nodded. "We're all here for him, no matter what it takes," he answered, and Maya and Dimitri agreed.

Chapter 7

Now

Charlotte changed into the jeans and sweatshirt quickly so as not to be gone if anything important happened. She and Becca were just stepping back into the waiting room when Pop returned. Charlotte could see evidence of tears on his face and wanted to put her arms around him, but she felt like that honor needed to come from Noah or Maya. As if reading her mind, both Greyson children embraced their Dad and then the strangest thing happened. The three of them stepped apart and motioned for Charlotte to join them.

"Come here Lottie," Pop ordered. "You're part of this family, too." Grabbing her locket for a quick prayer of thanks, she joined in the Greyson family group hug.

"Why don't you go in next, Sis?" Noah said to Maya. "You're our Mama Bear, right?" he asked as he smiled at his sister.

Maya gently touched his cheek but said with a smirk, "You'll pay for that when this is over."

Charlotte was filled with restless energy and couldn't sit down or even try to relax. Just because the Greysons considered her part of the family, would the hospital? Would she even get to go in to see Nick, and if she did, what would she do? She was still pacing and pondering when Maya came back and said it was Noah's turn.

Before leaving the waiting area he turned and looked at Charlotte, and she felt so helpless. *Shit, shit, shit!* she thought. I've got to be here for my friend Noah, but how do I do that when he's professed his love for me, knowing that I'm in love with his brother? *I guess I suck at all relationships with men*, were her last thoughts before Becca came to stand beside her.

"Hey Lottie," Becca asked softly, "what's going on in that redhead of yours?" More than anything, Charlotte needed to talk with Becca about Noah's admission, but she knew the time wasn't right. Instead she smiled weakly and replied, "Just thinking maybe I should call my Mom," she lied, but Becca could see right through her.

"I'll accept that for now," she told Charlotte, "but you and I are going to have a long talk real soon."

Charlotte gave her a nod and started pacing again. When Noah returned he was followed by the head nurse.

"Miss Luce," the nurse said to her, "are you ready to go back to see Agent Greyson?"

Charlotte followed her through the waiting room door and stopped as Nurse Bert turned to talk with her. "Our procedures say that only a wife or fiancé qualify as family at this point in a patient's care, but Mr. Greyson explained the situation, and both of his children told me that, in their hearts, you are family so I'm making an exception. Let's keep it our secret, okay?"

Charlotte wanted to put her arms around the compassionate caregiver, but she wasn't sure that was appropriate. Instead she just said, "Thank you," and followed her into Nick's room.

She didn't know what she had expected to see when she looked at Nick, but she wasn't at all prepared for the reality of it. It was obvious they had brought in some type of special bed to accommodate his six feet five-inch frame, but it still looked as if his feet were hanging off the bed. As her eyes moved cautiously up his body, it was all she could do to keep from keeling over at what she saw.

His beautiful face was puffy and swollen with bruises covering the right side. Tubes were coming out of his nose and his mouth, and she saw others that were draining fluid from his chest and his kidneys. His eyes were closed of course, but everything looked out of proportion and painful. "Oh Nick," she cried softly. "What have I done to you?"

Just then she felt a comforting hand on her shoulder as Shelly Bert asked her a question. "You love him very much, don't you?"

Trying to keep the tears from becoming sobs, Charlotte answered, "He's my whole world."

Chapter 8

Then

It was after one of Nick's swim meets in their junior year of high school that they started talking about their career goals for the future. Lottie was a whiz at math and loved working with numbers so she wanted to go into accounting or some other field that would allow her to utilize her skills.

"What about you, Nick?" she asked.

"Well, definitely something where I can keep swimming and maybe even coach. I love history so teaching and coaching kids would probably be my dream job. Of course, I never want to leave Anna Maria Island, it's the best place in the world to live."

The smile he gave her afterwards tugged at her heart, because as much as she loved AMI, she was headed off to Indiana and to Indiana University in a little over a year. Nick knew she was going to attend her dad's Alma Mater, but at that moment, it seemed a long way off.

Lottie had wanted to go to IU ever since she could remember. It's where her dad had attended college that spring break when he came to Anna Maria Island and met her mom. A week later he had headed back to school, not knowing he left his first love pregnant and alone, and with no premonition that a drunk driver would end his life before he made it back home.

Her gran was in Indiana, and so were all her plans, but when Lottie looked up at Nick, she realized her world was sitting right there beside her. She couldn't tell him that though so instead she said, "It sounds like a nice dream," and they headed off to Two Scoops for a victory sundae.

Chapter 9
Now

When Charlotte stepped back into the waiting room, she saw that everyone was gathered together, working on a plan. Stepping up beside Becca she asked, "What's up?"

Jared spoke first. "Becca needs to eat and to lay down for a while. I just suggested that maybe we should break up into teams and take turns going to lunch. That way someone will always be here if there's any change. I also think renting a couple of suites at the Radisson next door might be a good idea. Again, it would give you a place to go for some real rest, because I guarantee you this isn't going to be over in a day or two."

"I think that makes lots of sense, Jared," Pop responded. "I trust you know what we need to do, because to be honest, I think the rest of us are in over our heads. So why don't you take Lottie and Noah for a bite to eat, and Maya and Dimi can stay here with me. I'll call the hotel right now and make the reservations, and then Becca will have a place to take a nap after she eats."

"I'm not leaving you Pop," Noah stated firmly.

"And neither am I," Charlotte joined in. "So, Jared, please take your wife out for a break, but the rest of us are staying here."

"I don't really need to rest Jared," Becca chimed in, "but I am really hungry." Smiling sweetly at her husband she let him know she wasn't about to leave her friend.

Running his hands through his thick blond hair Jared sighed. "What do I know, I'm just a doctor," he said. "but I can tell when I'm out numbered. So instead, how about if I send out for some Jimmy Johns so we don't starve while we hold this waiting room vigil?"

Becca put her arms around him and pulled him in for a kiss, and the others all agreed with his new plan. "I still think renting a couple of suites is the right thing to do." Nodding his head, Pop agreed.

As the evening progressed more families settled in the waiting room, anxious for a word on their own loved one. As the Greyson party of family and friends huddled closer together, Jared was just about to try his hand at getting some of them to the hotel for rest when Shelly Bert stopped in to see them.

"I'm leaving for the night but I wanted to give you an update on Agent Greyson before I do. He's still sedated of course, and he appears to be resting comfortably. His vital signs are as well as can be expected, and I don't anticipate any problems overnight, but the night shift supervisor has my contact information if there are. Do you have any questions, or is there anything else I can do for you before I leave?"

Everyone shook their head except Pop who spoke up. "I can't tell you how much your kindness means to us Miss Bert. We all know how busy this hospital is, and your hands-on care has kept us going these past few hours."

She smiled at him and answered truthfully. "Your son and I are in the same line of work. We are both committed to protecting and taking care of the people we serve so giving him and his family a little extra TLC seems right. I do hope you all get some sleep tonight, and I'll see you early in the morning."

She started out the door and then turned back. "There's a chapel on the first floor," she offered. "Sometimes just being there brings me peace." And with that, she left.

Jared stood up and pulled Becca with him. "You heard the boss," he stated. "Now Dr. Tyler is gone and I'm speaking as my pregnant wife's husband, when I say that we're going to the hotel so she can get some sleep." He could see that Becca was about to protest when Charlotte grabbed her hand.

"Jared is right, Becca," she told her friend. "You need sleep and there's nothing you can do here tonight anyway. Please, go with Jared, and I'll see you tomorrow, okay?"

Giving Charlotte a hug, Becca moved towards her husband and said, "Okay."

Soon Dimitri and Maya left to call their girls and try to get some sleep leaving Pop, Noah, and Charlotte alone. Every time Charlotte looked up, she felt as if Noah was looking at her, and it made her feel sadder than she already was. After a few minutes of trying to find something to say, she finally spoke up.

"I'm going to find that chapel the nurse told us about," she said, "but I'll be back. Noah, you'll stay with Pop, won't you?" The last part she had thrown in so Noah wouldn't try to join her. She was thankful when he nodded his assent.

Reaching up for her locket, she silently communicated with Gran all the way to the first floor. Was she so clueless about men that she had been oblivious to Noah's feeling all these years just as she had been Nick's? She had always hoped Nick liked her for more than a friend, but Noah's revelation was turning her already jumpy stomach into a hot ball of hurt. She hadn't prayed in a long time, but she knew she owed God a long talk.

Chapter 10

Then

"Noah was suspended from school today," Nick told her as they were leaving after their last class of the day. "I know Pop is going to be pretty upset with him so maybe we shouldn't go to the marina."

Lottie was floored. "What!" she asked. "What in the world could he have done to get expelled from school? "

Nick sighed and stopped to look at her. Lottie never saw in herself what others did, especially guys, so he knew she wasn't going to understand. Truthfully, he didn't even want to tell her, but he knew she would hear it at school anyway, and he didn't want her to be unprepared.

"During gym class, he overheard a couple of guys talking about you and he didn't like it. He confronted them, and that's when they started getting a little vocal about…" Nick looked down so he wouldn't embarrass her, "your um, assets," he continued. "They started yelling and ended up in a real fight, and Coach Donavan had to break them up."

"Oh, my gosh, Nick," she cried. "Noah was suspended trying to defend my honor? Why would he do that? I'm used to the boys in this school being jerks, and the last thing I want is for Noah to get into trouble trying to protect me."

Lottie was crying in earnest now, and Nick didn't know how to make it better. He knew that Noah wanted her as much as he did, hell most of the guys in their class did, but he also knew that Noah would never do anything about it. They were brothers as well as friends, and Noah had known for a long time how Nick felt about Lottie Luce. It was just an unwritten rule that you didn't make a play for your brother's girl, even when she was oblivious to his feelings.

"Oh, you know Noah," he said, "probably mooning over a girl and took his frustration out the first opportunity he got." At least he wasn't totally lying to her, Nick thought.

Shaking her head Lottie responded, "It just doesn't make sense. Noah is one of the easiest going guys I've ever known, and he has girls from every different school in the district after him. There had to be another reason.

"I'm sure he's pretty embarrassed about the whole thing, so please don't say anything to him, Okay? Promise me you'll just let it go."

Lottie agreed not to talk to Noah about what had happened, but it broke her heart to know her friend was in so much trouble over a couple of loud-mouth boys. She tried her best not to call attention to her body, but some things just couldn't be easily hidden. Still, it didn't make sense that Noah would get in a fight over her.

Nick gave her a crooked grin and asked, "So, your place or Two Scoops?"

Chapter 11
Now

Saturday evening soon turned into Sunday morning, and Charlotte, Pop, and Noah were sleeping restlessly in chairs when Shelly Bert came back on duty. She was just about to leave them to their less than peaceful slumber when Charlotte woke up. Her eyes felt as if they were glued shut, and she was sure an army had been marching around in her mouth, but she managed a weak, "Good Morning."

"Good Morning, Miss Luce." Shelly answered her with a warm smile. "I just checked in on Agent Greyson, and there were no changes overnight. He looked just the same as when I left him yesterday, unfortunately I can't say the same for you," she teased. "I have a Keurig in my office and some Green Mountain dark, if you're interested. I promise you it's better than what you can get in the cafeteria and may help you feel a little more normal."

She motioned for Charlotte to follow her, and she did so eagerly feeling like a kid being offered a new pony! What was it about a good cup of coffee that could make everything look brighter?

"Now," Shelly said brightly. "The pods are in the basket over there, and I have both hazelnut and vanilla caramel creamer. Sometimes when I'm really stressed, I use both." The smile she gave Charlotte was so sincere that she felt some of the tension leave her body.

"I think the double shot is just what I need this morning," Charlotte told the compassionate nurse. "But I do need a favor. Will you please call me Charlotte? Miss Luce just sounds so old."

Shelly Bert nodded her head in agreement and replied, "Only if you'll call me Shelly." With a clink of their coffee cups, the two women each took a moment to savor the deep rich coffee, enjoying the mix of the sweet and creamy flavors.

The office was silent while the women relished their first cup of coffee for the day and then Shelly broke the silence. "I believe I heard Mr. Greyson rented a couple of rooms at the Radisson, right? I know you don't want to leave in case there's a change, but I promise you a hot shower will make you feel better and might help Agent Greyson as well."

Seeing the confused expression on Charlotte's face, the nurse continued. "We don't really know what's going on with a patient when they're in a coma," she said. "There is evidence that they are aware of scents and voices around them, even if they aren't strong enough to wake them up. When you go in to see Agent Greyson today, wouldn't you like to be clean and fresh and smelling like a rose? Well not literally," she laughed, "but they do have some really nice amenities at the Radisson, and yummy shower gel is one of them."

Charlotte could feel the tears welling up in her eyes, but this time she couldn't hold back her emotions. Pulling Shelly in for a hug she told her, "You are definitely an angel of mercy, Shelly, and I'm going to take your advice."

Swallowing the last of her coffee she headed to the waiting room to see if Pop and Noah were still sleeping or if Becca and Jared or Maya and Dimitri had returned.

Noah was sitting up, his head down, running his fingers through his dirty blond hair. When he saw Charlotte enter the room he smiled and motioned for her to sit down beside him. More than almost anything she wanted to run and hide, but seeing the pain in Noah's eyes, she knew she couldn't.

"How you holding up?" he asked her, reaching out to grab her hand.

Shit, shit, shit! she thought. Please don't let us have this conversation here. But instead she looked into his troubled face and responded honestly. "I feel like I'm in a dream," she told him, "and any moment the alarm's going to go off, and I'm going to need to get ready

24

for work. I want so much to be able to do something useful, and the feeling of helplessness is about to consume me."

"I get that," Noah said cautiously. "Nick has to recover, Lottie," Noah continued. "He's my big brother and my best friend, and next to Pop, he's the best man I know. I just wish the doctors would come back with some news. This waiting is pure agony."

Charlotte had just about decided to give him a hug when Pop woke up and thwarted her bad judgment. "Has there been any update?" he asked. At just that moment Shelly Bert came into the waiting room and spoke directly with Pop.

"Agent Greyson has been cleaned-up a little, so if you'd like to spend some time with him, it's fine. We're going to be more lenient on visitation today since he had such a good night, and I think it would do you good to see him. What do you think?"

Pop nodded and let the pretty nurse lead him in to the CCU. Charlotte explained her plan to go to the Radisson for a shower to Noah, and he nodded just as Maya and Dimi returned. Thankful that a heart-to-heart with him hadn't materialized, Charlotte gave a slight wave and headed to the elevators.

Chapter 12

Now

Shelly was right, the shower gel was amazing and after a long hot shower and shampoo, Charlotte emerged feeling as good as possible, considering. Thankful for the six pack of panties Becca brought her, Charlotte put on a clean pair, along with her wrinkled jeans and sweatshirt, and did her best to dry her long, thick hair. The only make-up she had in her purse was a ball of EOS coconut milk lip balm, and a tube of mascara; she applied both and headed back to the hospital.

Just as she reached the hotel lobby, Becca and Jared stepped out of the elevator holding hands. The glow on both of their faces told her that sleeping wasn't the only thing they had done last night, but Charlotte was okay with that. The parents of three active children, with a fourth on the way, didn't get much alone time, and she knew they needed it.

Not wanting to make a big deal out of her revelation, she smiled up at her friends and winked. Oddly enough it was Jared who seemed flustered, but it didn't bother her. She loved both Jared and Becca, and their happy marriage was the one hope she had that such a thing was possible. Wrapping her arm around their shoulders all she said was, "Good night, huh?" and the three of them walked out of the hotel back to check the status at the hospital.

Pop and Noah had both spent some time with Nick by the time she returned, and Shelly even allowed Maya and Dimitri to go in together for a few minutes. Pop explained Dimi needed to get home to the girls and the restaurant, but that Maya was going to stay, at least through the night. That meant once they were finished with their visit it would be her turn, and Charlotte was scared to death.

Maya stepped back into the waiting room and directly into her father's arms. Evidently there were times a girl still needed her dad, Charlotte thought wistfully, even when her strong handsome husband was standing by.

Shelly motioned for Charlotte and walked with her into Nick's room. To her, he looked the same as he had the day before, but Shelly assured her his color was better, and his breathing was less labored than on Saturday. Of course, he was still heavily sedated, but Shelly was pleased with his progress.

"The doctors will be in around one o'clock," she told a very nervous Charlotte, "but I'm hopeful for a good report. Now," she said steering Charlotte towards the bed, "get close to that man of yours and try to stimulate his senses. A light touch is okay too, just don't be expecting him to respond. I'm going to give you a few minutes of privacy, but then visiting time will be over." Giving Charlotte a soft squeeze on her arm, Shelly left the room, leaving Charlotte all alone with Nick and her thoughts.

"I'm so sorry Nick," she said as quietly as possible. "I wish I could take back all of the hateful things I said to you, but I can't, and I don't know how to make it better. Everyone is here, and we're all so scared, so please, come back to us." Using just the tips of her fingers she gently ran them over the side of his face that wasn't covered with bruises, and then without even thinking about it she gave his lips a soft kiss. "Can you smell the coconut?" she asked him. "I know it's your favorite."

Feeling a tap on her back she turned and there was Shelly, ready to take her back to Nick's family and another long day playing the waiting game.

By two o'clock everyone was feeling pretty antsy, as they waited for the doctors to appear. Just when Charlotte thought she couldn't sit quietly another minute, both Dr. Copeland and Dr. Rivers came into the waiting room.

"Mr. Greyson," Dr. Copeland addressed Pop, while looking at the group of Nick's family and friends. "Dr. Rivers and I have just performed an extensive examination and evaluation of Agent Greyson, and we both are pleased with the results. The incision from the gunshot wound shows no sign of infection and is draining nicely." Looking over at Dr. Rivers, she allowed him to continue.

"The swelling on his brain hasn't changed since yesterday, but that's not a bad thing because it means it hasn't gotten worse. We've agreed to keep him in an induced coma until Tuesday morning, and then barring any complications, we'll start weaning him from the medication."

Trying to stay strong Maya spoke-up. "How long until he wakes up?" she asked, her voice shaky and quivering.

"I wish I had an answer for you," Dr. Rivers said with a kind smile, "but every case is different. Since we'll be cutting the medication back slowly so we can monitor his responses, I would say Thursday or Friday at the very earliest."

Dr. Copeland took over from there. "The one thing Agent Greyson is going to need most is a strong, healthy support system, so I encourage you all to get a good meal and a good night's sleep. Miss Bert and the rest of the CCU team have your cell numbers, and I promise you they'll call if there are any changes. I know you think you need to stay here in case you're needed, but as much as I hate to tell you this, at this point, you're not. So please, get out of here for a while and take care of you."

As soon as the doctors left, the group sat back down, almost as if they hadn't heard a word she had said. Standing up, holding on to Becca's arm, Jared approached Charlotte. "We hate to leave you here, but I have to be in the clinic tomorrow, and Becca needs to see the kids. We'll call you as soon as we get back to New Smyrna, and you can call either one of us anytime if you need to, okay? Please get some rest Charlotte, you're going to scare Nick when he wakes up if you look like that."

Seeing the smile and the warmth in his eyes, Charlotte agreed, and told them to go home. She and Becca hugged for a long time, and then Charlotte's friends walked out the door. Her heart was hurting, but she knew they had to go, so she decided it was time to call her mom.

Just as she was about to share her plan with Nick's family, Director James came into the waiting room. "We have a person of interest," he told them all, "and every law enforcement officer in the state is on the lookout for him."

"Who is it?" asked Noah.

"Kid by the name of Adam Jennings," he replied. "He fits the description given by Nick's neighbor, and I just found out today that he somehow walked away from the minimum-security prison in Pensacola."

"Isn't he the guy that Nick arrested in the Stella Harper stalking case? Why in the world after all he put that girl through was he in a minimum-security prison?"

"Yes, Nick was the agent who finally captured Jennings after a cross continent chase, but we only arrest them, it's up to someone else to prosecute and sentence." It was obvious that Director James was not a happy camper so no one else questioned what was being done to find Adam Jennings.

Holding up a set of keys he told Pop, "We've completed our crime scene search of Nick's condo, so you and your family are welcome to use it as a home base, unless for some reason you think he would object. I've also brought his Jeep so you'll have transportation back and forth."

Pop took the keys and thanked the deputy director for his time and information. "You'll keep us informed on the investigation, right?" he asked.

"You'll know just as soon as we do," he responded. "Any update on Nick's condition?"

Pop told him all that they knew, and as soon as the director left, they began to make their plans.

"How about we all go get some dinner and then I drop the three of you off at Nick's, and I take the Jeep back to Anna Maria?" Noah asked. "My boat's supposed to come in tomorrow, and I can check out the marina while I'm there. If there aren't any changes, I'll be back on Tuesday."

At this point they were all starving. Pop, Maya, and Charlotte agreed, although leaving Nick was hard for all of them. Charlotte took a moment to let Shelly know their plans and to make sure she had their cell phone numbers, and then with a full heart, Charlotte walked away with the others.

Chapter 13

Now

Even after some real food and a night in a real bed, the trio returned to the hospital on Monday morning, still running on auto-pilot. Shelly beat them in and was waiting with a big smile when they got to the hospital.

"Good morning," she said sweetly. "How was your night away?"

The looks she received from Pop and Charlotte gave her the answer so she switched tactics. "Agent Greyson had a very good night," she told them. "I'm very pleased with his progress. Why don't you come into my office and get a cup of real coffee while the nurses give him his bath, and then we can start a visiting rotation? I stopped at the bakery and picked up some fresh muffins, too, in case you're hungry."

Charlotte was in awe of the warm and caring spirit Shelly exuded and thought if she was about ten years younger she'd be perfect for Noah. He needed a decent woman in his life, but she was pretty sure Shelly was in her early forties and at twenty-nine, that seemed like too much of an age difference for him. And to be honest, she didn't know if Shelly was even available. She said she was Miss Bert, but that could still mean she had a boyfriend or fiancé. She decided right then though that she wanted to know more about the sweet blonde nurse who was going out of her way to make their life more comfortable.

The coffee was just what the doctor ordered, and today Shelly had added Chocolate Toffee Truffle to her selection of creamers. "Yum," Charlotte moaned, "this is so good."

"I'm glad that you like it," Shelly responded with a smile. "Now, I have a question for you. Agent Greyson is definitely sporting more than a five o'clock shadow, do you want the nurse to shave him, would you like to shave him, or do we let it go?"

Charlotte looked at Pop for direction, not feeling that this should be her call. "That's a decision a woman needs to make," he laughed. "I don't care one way or another."

Shelly agreed so she offered a solution. "How about I take Charlotte in to see him and she can decide. Are you okay with that Maya?"

Maya nodded her consent and Shelly and Charlotte headed to Nick's room. Just before they entered Charlotte stopped and asked Shelly a question. "Are you available for lunch or dinner today?" she asked her. "I'd really like to get to know you better."

Shelly blushed as she answered. "I'd like that very much. How about dinner when I get off at six o'clock?"

"It's a date," Charlotte told her, and she stepped into Nick's room.

Chapter 14

Now

Charlotte had never known Nick with anything but a clean-shaven face so she was caught off guard by how quickly his dark beard had grown in. "*How did I miss this yesterday?*" she questioned herself but decided the stress of the situation was the culprit.

Nick had always been meticulous about his appearance so Charlotte was struggling with the decision about whether to shave him. The beard gave him a sexy roguish look and combined with the dark bruise growing on his cheek, he almost had a bad boy appeal about him. Charlotte suppressed a giggle at the thought of Nick as a bad boy and decided the beard needed to go. Too many pretty young women worked in this department, and she wanted no part of enticing them!

"If you're sure its okay, I'd like to shave him," she told Shelly, "but I hope you'll stay nearby if I need help."

Shelly nodded her agreement and helped Charlotte get started. Thirty minutes and only one small cut later, Nick looked more like himself, and once again, Charlotte was faced with a day of waiting for answers.

Maya stepped outside to call Dimi and the twins, leaving Charlotte and Pop alone. She thought he looked as if he had aged ten years in the past two days, and her heart ached for him. The man who had been such an amazing father to his own kids, had been more than an amazing role model to her, and she wished more than ever she had stayed in contact with him after she and Nick had their falling out. Laying her head back on the couch she closed her eyes, and memories of the important times Pop had been there through her childhood started running through her head.

Chapter 15
Then

Lottie had felt odd for the last few days, but there weren't any symptoms she could put her finger on. Her mom took a part time job at Publix to help augment her income from the jewelry she made, and Lottie didn't want to put more on her plate so she kept quiet. Becca was on vacation with her family so when Nick invited her to spend the day swimming and kayaking with him and Noah, she immediately said yes. It was the summer she turned eleven, and she was stuck somewhere between a little girl and a young woman.

After a morning on the water and a lunch of bologna sandwiches and chips, Lottie's stomach felt a little off so she snuck into the bathroom while the boys were cleaning up. She didn't feel sick, just maybe a little crampy, but she was not at all prepared to see the spots of blood in her bathing suit when she sat down on the toilet. She had learned all about having periods from her health class at school, and her mom had even added a little more insight to the process of becoming a woman, but she wasn't expecting it anytime soon, and especially not when she was at the marina with Nick and his brother!

Tears started to well up in her eyes, and she couldn't think straight. Her mom didn't get off work for hours and even if she decided to walk home, what would she do once she got there, and what excuse could she give Nick for leaving? Pulling her bathing suit back up and wishing she had brought clothes to change into, she heard a soft knock at the door.

"Lottie, are you okay?" Pop asked. "The boys went back outside, and I'm worrying about you."

Not knowing what to say, Lottie opened the bathroom door and the tears fell in earnest. How did she tell a man, a man who was not her dad, what was going on? But it turned out she didn't need to.

"You know, Lottie," he said gently, "when Maya was just about your age we had to make a trip to Walgreens late one night for some female supplies. Do you and I need to make a run to town?"

Lottie nodded her head, too humiliated to look him in the eye, but thankful just the same for his kindness. "Come on," Pop said. "We'll tell the boys were going out to get some ice cream, and they'll never be the wiser."

Chapter 16

Now

Charlotte sat up and took a good look at the man who had helped her through one of the most intimate experiences in a girl's life. Reaching over, she took his hand and looked at his weary blue eyes. "I've never thanked you for everything you did for me while I was growing up," she told him. "You were one of the most important people in my life."

Pop smiled at her and leaned in to kiss her cheek. "You've always been like a daughter to me, Lottie, and that will never change. I pray when Nick wakes up the two of you can resolve your issues, but regardless, you'll always have a place in my heart and in my home."

Throwing her arms around his neck she whispered in his ear, "I pray that, too."

When Shelly got off at six o'clock, Charlotte was more than ready for a break. The visits to Nick's room were short and few between, and every time she saw him she was reminded of how cruel she had been the last time they were together. Yes, he had hurt her badly, but she had acted like a child with her retaliation, and as each day passed, she worried she might never have an opportunity to tell him. Having dinner with Shelly and getting to know her better was just what she needed.

"There's a great Italian place around the corner from the hospital," she told Charlotte. "I have my car if you'd rather go somewhere else?"

"I love Italian," Charlotte told her new friend, "and I'd really like to stay close to the hospital in case Pop needs me. Am I dressed okay? I've been wearing these jeans for three days now, but my options are kind of limited."

"You look fine Charlotte, and trust me, Antonio's gets lots of business from the hospital, so please don't worry about it." Her face was so kind and supportive that Charlotte had to agree.

The waiter showed them to a booth and offered a wine list, but both women declined. After deciding on the special of the day, chicken picatta with risotto and an antipasto salad, Charlotte asked Shelly about her life, and why she had become a nurse.

"It's really a long story," she said, stopping to take a sip of sparkling water. "I always wanted to be a kindergarten teacher and was actually in my second year of a BS in Early Childhood Education when life changed my plans."

"What happened," Charlotte teased. "Did you meet a guy?"

Shelly swirled the water in her glass for a few seconds before answering. "No, she said," looking down at the table instead of at Charlotte. "I lost one."

Charlotte felt her stomach turn as Shelly shared with her the story of her fiancé Sam, and how he had died from a friendly fire accident while serving in the marines. They had been together since they were in the eighth grade and their wedding was planned for Sam's next leave. Shelly was just twenty years old when he died, and for eighteen months afterwards, she had totally quit living and grieved.

"I might have stayed in my little cocoon of pain, but my mom got sick and she needed me. She had a stroke when she was just forty-two years old, and she was never the same afterwards. She needed almost full-time care, and my dad's job as a long-haul trucker didn't allow him the time to stay with her or the money to hire someone else. So, I went from being a happily engaged college student to a woman consumed with grief to my mom's caretaker within two years, but being with her, is what really made me examine my priorities."

Charlotte was numb. She had allowed the circumstances of her life and relationship with Nick to result in years of self-pity, and now she felt nothing but shame. Taking Shelly's hand in her own she whispered, "I'm so sorry," as she tried to hold back the tears.

"Please don't cry for me Charlotte," she said with a smile. "My life had some bumps in the road it's true, but it also led me to a nursing degree and a job I love so very much. Helping families like yours is what gets me out of bed every day. I still miss Sam and my mom more than I can tell you, but I'm at peace, and that's the best place to be."

They stayed at the restaurant for hours, talking about everything under the sun, and when Shelly finally said she had to call it a night, both women knew they had found a good friend. Charlotte stroked her locket as they walked back to the hospital, and when Shelly headed to the parking garage, Charlotte talked to her Gran.

"Gran, it's me, Lottie," she began. "I really miss you, but I've made a new friend and she reminds me of you. She's had a lot of heartbreak, and just like you, she always manages a smile."

Chapter 17

Now

The next afternoon Dimi surprised Maya by bringing the girls to see her. While they enjoyed cookies from the vending machine, Charlotte decided to walk down to the gift shop to see if they had any clothing options for sale. Much to her delight, she was able to buy a pair of leggings and a breast cancer awareness T-shirt so she could finally get out of her jeans! She mentally planned on doing a load of laundry at Nick's condo when Pop came to get her.

"I just wanted to let you know that the doctors were just by and they've started weaning Nick off the sedative," he told her excitedly. "Just think, in a day or two, he'll be awake and this nightmare can go away."

He looked so hopeful that Charlotte wasn't about to tell him that the doctors had said Nick might start to regain consciousness in a day or two, not that he would. *It's still a beginning*, she thought, and maybe Nick would wake-up soon and his healing process could begin.

But that was not to be the case. Every morning Charlotte started her day with coffee in Shelly's office followed by a visit with Nick. She talked to him, she caressed him, but there was no change in his condition.

Shelly was off on Saturday, and when she returned on Sunday, it was to a very tired and stressed family. She once again invited Charlotte in for her cup of morning coffee, but when Shelly handed her the cup, Charlotte backed away, the aroma made her feel ill.

"Are you okay, Charlotte?" Shelly questioned. "I've never seen you turn up your nose at coffee."

"We had Chinese last night," Charlotte replied. "I think maybe the hot and sour soup didn't set well with me."

"That's because its gross," Shelly laughed. "I always think it looks like hot snot!"

Just the verbal image was enough to send Charlotte running to the bathroom. After losing the toast and orange juice she had eaten in the cafeteria, she sat down in Shelly's office, shaky and embarrassed.

"I'm so sorry," she apologized. "I never get sick, but maybe I really have a bug, or the stress of Nick not coming around has gotten to me worse than I thought." Putting her face in her hands, she willed the tears not to fall.

"Have you tried telling him?" Shelly asked gently.

"Telling him wh-what?" Charlotte replied.

"About the baby, Charlotte. Maybe it's time you told Agent Greyson that you're pregnant."

The room was totally quiet and Shelly spoke again. "I've been a nurse a long time my friend, and I know the symptoms. I've watched you napping every chance you get, your hand protectively over your tummy, and when you aren't sleeping, you're off to the bathroom. But not being able to stomach the smell of coffee was the clincher."

Charlotte started to cry while Shelly patted her hand. "How about I get a pregnancy test from the drugstore next door over my lunch hour, and we'll find out for sure, okay?"

Charlotte agreed weakly as she wiped away her tears with the back of her hand. "What am I going to do if it's positive?" she asked.

"Well, you're going to have some decisions to make, but Agent Greyson needs to be a part of them, don't you agree? And if it is positive, that just might be the incentive his brain needs to quit sleeping and wake-up."

Chapter 18
Now

After an unbelievably long morning, Shelly found time to take her lunch break while Charlotte worked herself up into a tizzy. *Shit, shit, shit!* she thought. *Can this situation get any more complicated?*

What if she was pregnant? What if Nick never recovered, or what if he did, but he wanted nothing to do with her or their baby? She knew nothing about being a mother, her own mother had been just a teenager when she was born. How could she raise a child, or did she even want to? The questions were making her head ache so she closed her eyes and almost jumped out of her chair when Shelly touched her shoulder.

"Um, Charlotte, do you have a minute?" she asked, walking towards her office. Charlotte felt as if she was glued to her seat, and it took every ounce of her strength to pull herself out of the chair. At this moment, she wanted nothing more than to be an ostrich and stick her head in the sand!

Shelly had the test waiting for her in the bathroom and gently guided Charlotte towards it. "This test can detect pregnancy less than forty-eight hours after conception, so since you've been here over a week, it should be accurate. Go on Charlotte," she prodded, "It's the not knowing that's driving you crazy." With one of her warm and caring smiles, Shelly led Charlotte into the bathroom and showed her the instructions.

"It's almost foolproof," she told a very nervous Charlotte, "and I'll be waiting right here."

After ten-minutes and no sound from the bathroom, Shelly knocked on the door. "How are you doing in there?" she asked, but there was no response. "Charlotte, I'm coming in if you don't open the door right now so I hope you have your pants pulled up."

The door opened slowly, and the tear stained face of her friend stood before here. "Oh honey," Shelly comforted her. "Are those tears of joy or sorrow?"

"I don't know," Charlotte sobbed, "but you're a very good nurse Miss Bert, because according to this little stick, I'm definitely pregnant." She felt herself being pulled into the arms of her new friend, and she stayed there feeling safe, at least for the moment.

"So, Charlotte, what happens next?" Shelly asked. "Are you ready to tell Agent Greyson; or maybe you need to talk with your mom or Dr. Tyler's wife first?"

Shaking her head Charlotte said quietly, "Nick needs to be the first to know, but I can't tell him until I have a better handle on my feelings. I'm unemployed and I just committed a boatload of money to help a friend. This probably isn't a great time to think about bringing a child into my life. Besides, with my track record with relationships, I had pretty much decided that my career was going to be my baby. And look at what a good job I did with that." Remembering her split with Olde Florida brought the tears back in full force.

Shelly sighed and took Charlotte's hand. "Sit down and talk with me," she said. "I don't want to sway your decision, Charlotte, but I need to share a story with you before you make up your mind."

Charlotte dried her tears and sat down on the sofa beside Shelly, her hand automatically resting on her stomach.

"I was raised in a very conservative home," Shelly began. "As soon as my parents could tell that Sam and I were serious about each other, my mom sat me down and told me that sex was to be reserved for marriage. We went to church every Sunday morning and every Wednesday night, and our faith was very strong about the roles of men and women. I was an only child, and I loved my parents and respected their values, and I made sure Sam knew them as well. It didn't mean he liked them, but he loved me and he agreed to wait. Six years is a long time when you're young and in love, so the night before Sam was to deploy, I decided I wanted to give him something of mine to take with him, and I gave him myself."

Shelly stopped for a moment, obviously reliving the moment, allowing Charlotte to remember the last time with Nick. He had been sound asleep when she had taken him in her mouth. "Think of this as a parting gift," she had told him when he roared to life, but it was in his response that their baby had been conceived.

"I'll show you a parting gift," he had told her, lifting her on to his throbbing erection, and they had made love without using protection. What is it about wanting to give a man a special gift?

"Anyway," Shelly resumed, "I, naturally, was not on birth control, and Sam wasn't prepared either, so we tried the old-fashioned method, which obviously, is harder than it sounds. By the time I found out I was pregnant, Sam was in the Middle East, and I didn't want him to worry about me when he was so far away; and I couldn't bear to shame my family, so I had an abortion. Sam was killed just a few weeks later, never knowing about our baby. For a long time, I thought God was punishing me for having premarital sex, and then having an abortion, which is a big part of the wall of grief I built around myself."

Charlotte spoke for the first time. "Surely you know God doesn't work that way Shelly?"

"I do now," she answered. "It doesn't change the fact that I not only lost Sam, but I killed the only part of him I had left. I got rid of my chance to be a mother Charlotte, and I don't want you to have that same regret. You have plenty of time to think about what's best for you and your life, but I beg you, don't make any decision until you really think it through, and can talk to Agent Greyson first."

Chapter 19
Then

Jared stepped out of the delivery room dressed in scrubs, but for once he was the patient and not the doctor. "It's a boy, Lottie, "he told her with tears in his eyes. "Becca and I have a son."

The new father and his wife's best friend hugged before she started pelting him with questions.

"Is everyone okay?" she asked. "How much did he weigh and what's his name? I just can't believe that Becca is a mommy."

"Yes, mother and baby are both doing fine, although Becca is pretty worn out. It was a long labor, but she was so strong. Weight was eight pounds two ounces, and he was twenty-one inches long, but as of yet he has no name. We had a couple picked out, but Becca isn't feeling so sure about either one right now."

"When can I see them?" Lottie asked eagerly. "I'm not sure I've ever been close to a brand-new person."

Jared laughed at her description of his son, but he took her arm and led her towards his family. "Becca's mom and my mom are on their way," Jared told her. "You get to be the first to see Baby Boy Tyler. Please don't tell them that though or they'll both make my life a living hell!"

When Charlotte walked into the room she was overcome with an emotion she had never experienced. Her friend, her sister by everything but blood, was propped up in the hospital bed, holding a tiny blue bundle, her face aglow with a serenity Charlotte had never seen.

Becca held out her hand and guided Charlotte beside the bed. "Meet Jared Daniel Tyler, Jr," she said as the tears formed in her eyes.

"I took one look at him and just knew he was a miniature version of his dad."

Jared stepped to the other side of the bed and put his arms around his family. "Are you sure, Becca?" he asked her, obviously overjoyed about her decision. "We never discussed naming a boy after me."

"He couldn't have any other name, Jared, just look at him. But, I was thinking we might call him JD, just to save the confusion of two Jared's in the house. What do you think?"

The smile on Jared's face said it all, and Charlotte almost felt like she was intruding on a private moment when Becca spoke up. "Would you like to hold him, Auntie Lottie?" she asked, "after all, I'm going to expect lots of diaper changing from you."

Charlotte paled. "I've never changed a diaper in my life Rebecca Rose Huddleston Tyler," she said, "but give me this little guy because I'm ready to learn!"

Chapter 20
Now

Charlotte stepped out of Shelly's office in a daze. "How could one person deal with so much sorrow?" she asked herself.

Shelly was the epitome of sunshine and happiness, yet she had lost the only man she had ever loved when she was hardly more than a girl, and she'd carried a secret with her for over twenty years that would cripple most women. It was right then that Charlotte knew what she needed to do.

"Ok, Special Agent," she said to herself. "It's time you and I had a talk."

After the doctor's rounds and Pop and Maya's visits with Nick, she gathered her courage and made her way into his room. The beep, beep of the machines reminded her that Nick was still very critical, but everyday his color looked better, and the swelling in his face was going down.

A five o'clock shadow covered his jaw and Charlotte decided this time she would leave it. She knew Nick would never feel it was professional to go to work with any kind of facial hair, but he wasn't at work right now, was he?

Sitting down beside him on the bed, she began stroking his face which she had started doing every day. She kept hoping he would remember her touch and give her a sign, but so far there was nothing. Gently she kissed his lips and trying not to cry, she spoke.

"I'm here Nick, and I've been every day since you were hurt. I've apologized and I've talked with you, but I'm not sure I ever said what it was I came to this hospital to say. I love you, too, Nick, I've always loved you, and I need you to wake-up because I have some news to share." Charlotte took a deep breath and watched his face to see if she could see any recognition, but there wasn't any. Letting out a big sigh she started again.

"Remember our last night together, when we made love without protection? We were both afraid the other would be worried about an STD, but we never even discussed the birth control side of that equation. So, evidently, I forgot to get a shot after Peter and I broke-up.... Wait, forget I said that, so the thing is, Nick, I'm pregnant. I'm going to have a baby, we're going to have a baby, and I'm so scared. I need to know that you aren't mad at me, and that you forgive me, and you still love me, but most of all I need you to want this baby as much as I do, because I do want it, I really, really do."

Chapter 21
Now

That evening Charlotte discovered a stackable washer and dryer in Nick's condo and set out to get the few belongings she had with her clean. Maya had decided to go home overnight with her family, and Noah had returned from the island, so Pop and Noah said they would take the twin beds in the guest room, and Charlotte could take the master. She smiled as she thought about the two large grown men sleeping in the pink room, decorated with fairies and butterflies for Nick's two nieces' visits, but the thought of sleeping in Nick's bed terrified her.

After folding her clean clothes and eating the take-out salad Pop had brought her, Charlotte ventured into Nick's room. It was masculine, without a bachelor pad vibe, and she could feel Nick as soon as she stepped inside. The bed was unmade and rumpled after Pop slept there, so she decided to strip the sheets and make it up fresh. As she picked up a pillow to pull off the case, she couldn't help but put it to her face to breathe in the unmistakable smell of Nick. Citrus and spice, and one-hundred percent male, she experienced a very unexpected rush of longing and decided that at least that pillowcase would remain unwashed.

The sheets were clean and back on the bed, and Charlotte was faced with two options. Pop had already turned in so she could either sit in the living room, alone with Noah, which she wasn't ready for, or go to bed herself and face the ghosts of women past who had slept there with Nick. Neither choice was a good one, but she was tired herself and decided to call it a night.

The bed was huge, a California king to accommodate Nick's long frame, and despite being five-foot ten herself, Charlotte felt dwarfed by its size. She tossed and turned, while holding her Nick infused pillow, and tried not to think about Nick's life here in Tampa. How many women had Nick brought to this bed? How many of them had he been in love with or thought he would have a future with? She knew those thoughts were counterproductive to a good night's sleep, but here in Nick's room, surrounded by images of a life she had never been a part of, it was all she could think about. *Maybe talking with Noah would have been the better option*, she thought, trying to keep the tears from falling that seemed to be following her around.

Eventually she fell asleep, dreaming she lived in the condo with Nick, but she and their child slept in the little girl inspired guest room while he paraded a different woman in front of her, and into his bed, every night. When she finally woke-up it was seven o'clock a.m., and she still felt as tired as when she first laid down. Voices from the other room let her know that Pop and Noah were awake so she quickly got out of bed and headed to the shower.

The thought of fresh, clean clothes was intoxicating, and she was just about to step into the walk-in shower when she was overcome by a wave of nausea. Morning sickness, are you freaking kidding me? she asked herself after hanging over the toilet for several minutes. *Shit, shit, shit! I've got to get myself under control.*

Pop and Noah were dressed and ready to go when Charlotte walked into the kitchen. "I'm starving," said Noah. "How about if we stop at McDonalds on the way in for a steak and egg bagel and a hot cup of coffee? That stuff Shelly makes is a little too fru fru for my tastes."

The thought of food just about sent Charlotte running back to the bathroom, but somehow, she was able to contain the whitecaps rolling around in her stomach.

"Um, no McDonalds for me, thanks," she said, trying to keep it together, "but there's a 7-Eleven right on the way and I would love a 7-Up and some peanut butter cheese crackers. Would you mind if we stopped?"

"Now Lottie," Pop said sternly, "don't tell me you're on some kind of diet again. Why, you look like you've lost weight just while we've been here, and you were too thin anyway if you ask me."

Charlotte gave Nick's dad a genuine smile. "I'm not trying to lose weight, I promise, but I haven't been sleeping very well so I thought I'd try cutting back on caffeine." The dark circles under her eyes should back her up, even if it wasn't the true reason she was giving up coffee.

On the drive in, Noah caught them up-to-date on what was happening on Anna Maria Island and even told Charlotte how much people missed her at the bank. "I had more than one of your former employees, and several customers, tell me how different the bank is without you, Shortcake. I sure hope the powers that be knew what they were doing."

Charlotte smiled to herself, thankful her presence in the bank was missed and that Noah had called her by his pet name, Shortcake! Maybe his declaration of love wasn't going to affect their friendship after all.

While Noah ran in to get breakfast for him and his dad, Charlotte decided to check her email. She'd pretty much turned her phone off when they first arrived at the hospital, but with a few minutes to kill she had an opportune time. The first thing she saw was five missed calls from Peter as well as four unopened emails. *Shit, shit, shit! This was not good! Talking to Peter with Pop and Noah so close was not an option* so she scrolled through the rest of her messages and decided to wait for a more private time to call him back.

Noah returned with a bag of greasy food, and Charlotte was pretty sure she turned green. Thankfully, the Seven Eleven was right up the block, and when they got there, she bolted out of the Jeep, almost before it came to a complete stop. After three crackers and a small sip of 7-Up she was feeling better and headed back outside. A deep breath of early morning air also helped her queasy stomach, but when she got back into the Jeep, Noah looked at her strangely.

"You sure you're okay, Lottie?" he asked. "Something just seems a little off."

"Maybe it's because I've spent over a week sitting in the hospital waiting for your brother to wake-up, and I've lost my job and my whole world is falling apart," she said a little more forcefully than she meant to. "Now, please, will you both stop fussing over me and just drive? We're already way later than usual, and I'm sure Shelly is wondering where we are."

Noah gave her a salute, as if to say, "Yes ma'am" but the look he gave his dad proved he wasn't thoroughly convinced.

Chapter 22

Now

While Noah parked, Charlotte decide to call Peter. "You go on ahead, Pop," she told Nick's dad. "I need to make a phone call but I won't be long." Pop nodded and headed for the elevator, and Charlotte stepped outside to make her call.

"Charlotte, thank God, I've been so worried. Where are you, are you all right?" Peter asked.

"I'm in Tampa, Peter," she told him, trying not to sound cross. She and Peter may not be a couple any longer, but she wanted to keep him as a friend. "Surely you've heard by now that Nick was shot at his condo? I'm here at the hospital with his dad and brother. Is something going on?"

Peter let out a big sigh before continuing. "Yes, I heard about Nick, Charlotte, and I'm truly sorry. The word on the island is it doesn't look good for his recovery, is that true?"

Charlotte's blood was boiling! Surely Peter wasn't going to use this to try worm his way back into her life, was he? She wouldn't date him again for any reason, but Nick was improving every day, no matter what the island gossip thought.

"Thankfully you've been misinformed, Peter, but surely you had a reason to call and leave so many messages?" *There Gran, are you proud of me*, she silently asked her grandmother as she reached up to touch her locket. *I can keep my temper under control.*

"Yes, of course I had a reason," Peter replied gruffly. "Owen Gardner has been trying to get hold of you but the only number he has is for your landline. He asked me to have you call him, but apparently, my calls are not a priority."

"Peter, please, I've not been ignoring you but the hospital has a strict policy about cell-phone use, and honestly, my focus has been on Nick and his family. I appreciate you getting hold of me, and I'll call Owen right away. I don't want to fight with you, so please understand."

"I do understand, Charlotte. I understand only too well. Goodbye."

Charlotte felt sick and not from the pregnancy this time. Hurting Peter was the last thing she wanted to do, but she had to be honest with him, right? Dialing the number she had for Owen Gardner, she prayed whatever he had to say to her was good news.

"Owen Gardner," came the voice on the other end of the phone, and Charlotte let out the breath she had been holding the entire time she dialed.

"Hi, Owen, this is Charlotte Luce," she spoke into the phone, "and I hear you've been trying to reach me."

"Charlotte, finally," he laughed. "I thought maybe you'd fallen off the face of the earth. When Peter couldn't get you either I was really concerned."

Hmm, just what had Peter told Owen about their relationship, she wondered? She would have liked to get some answers but she knew Pop and Noah were waiting for her upstairs.

"Peter and I are old friends," she told him, "but I'm out of town and he didn't know that. What's up; news about Carol, I hope?"

"Great news, actually. She's been released and the charges against her have been dropped. Tony totally rolled over on the thugs he'd been working for, but now we have a different problem." Owen stopped for a moment to let everything sink in. "Carol can't go back to the Island, Charlotte, and while I have her in a safe place for now, I don't know how long she'll be able to stay there. The men Tony was working for are bad guys, so she's going to have to make some radical changes in her life."

"I can't thank you enough for getting her out of there, Owen, but I'm not sure what you're asking of me. Is it money you need, or what?"

"At this moment, nothing, but Carol is going to need someplace to go, and I was hoping you might have an idea. Any chance your contact with the FBI would be willing to put her into witness protection?"

"I don't really have a contact with the FBI, Owen, but if she's willing to go, I may know a place in Arizona that's both remote, and private. I can't make any promises, and I may not have an answer today, but I'll work on it, okay?"

"You're a good friend, Charlotte Luce, too bad my old buddy Peter let you slip away."

Charlotte wasn't sure how to answer so she just told him goodbye and that he'd be hearing from her. Because right now though, she needed to see her contact in the FBI!

Chapter 23

Now

Charlotte was full of nervous energy as she waited for the elevator to arrive. Carol was free, the charges had been dropped, and now all she needed to do was see if her mom would be willing to harbor her for a while. It didn't seem like too much to ask, did it? But first, she needed to check with Shelly to see how Nick was, and if by some miracle, her words had made their way into his still swollen and sleeping brain.

After a short ride on the elevator, that seemed much longer, Charlotte stepped off on the Critical Care floor, and was taken back by how quiet the waiting room was. Where was Pop and Noah, and where was her friend Shelly? Her office was empty, and there was no sign of life, and Charlotte began to panic.

Moving slowly down the hall she saw that the door to Nick's room was closed and it was all she could do not to fall. Reaching up for the strength of her locket she silently prayed to her grandmother. "Oh, please, Gran," she whispered reverently, "please don't let there be something wrong. Nick was doing so well, and I thought telling him about the baby might help, and oh yeah, Gran, I guess I'm following in my mom's footsteps after all, because I'm pregnant. But truly all that matters right now is Nick."

She was just about to go back to the waiting room when Shelly stepped out of his room. "Oh, Charlotte, there you are," Shelly sighed. "Around three o'clock this morning Nick started to become agitated and so far, nothing we've done has helped. He isn't coherent by any means, but Dr. Rivers says that if we can't get him calmed down in the next thirty minutes he's going to have to sedate him again, and none of us want that. His dad and brother have both tried talking him down, but it isn't working, are you up for a try?"

Charlotte felt the air going out of her chest and knew she was about five seconds from blacking out. She'd had such high hopes for this day, and now everything was going wrong. Shelly put her arm around her and holding her up said, "Breathe, Charlotte. You need to breathe."

When they were sure she wasn't going to do a face plant, Charlotte nodded and let the gentle nurse guide her into Nick's room. Her heart caught in her throat when she saw that he had been put in restraints to keep from pulling out a tube or hurting himself, and the indignity was almost more than she could bear. Had her news done this to him? Shelly guided her towards the bed and whispered in her ear, "Let him know that you're here, Charlotte."

Looking at Nick was like looking at someone unable to wake up from a bad dream, which to be honest, she told herself, he was. Carefully getting as close to the bed as possible, she stroked his face and talked to him as if he were a child, lost and afraid.

"I'm right here, Nick," she told him. "Everything is going to be okay, so just relax. I'm not going to leave you." Over and over she repeated her mantra, stroking his face and arms and even lightly kissing his forehead, and little by little, his body stopped jerking and twitching and gave in to the comfort of her voice. Pop was in the corner, trying not to cry, and Noah had his arm around his dad, his face drawn and pale.

When Shelly saw Nick's blood pressure and pulse were back to normal, she laid her hand on Charlotte's shoulder. "You did good, friend," she smiled. "I think you can rest now." However, there was no way Charlotte was going to stop. She could stay here and reassure Nick all day and night, if that's what it took, but leaving his side was no longer an option.

Chapter 24

Now

After three hours of soothing Nick with light reassuring caresses and words, Charlotte felt as if her bladder would burst! She knew the patient's bathrooms were supposed to be off limits to visitors, but honestly, who would know? It's not as if Nick was using it, right? Always good at multitasking, she grabbed her bottle of 7-Up and crackers from the chair by her purse, and quietly took them into the bathroom with her.

"Ah," Charlotte sighed as she both let out and put in liquid, and then, just because it felt so good to sit down, she took an extra minute to inhale three more crackers and take a big gulp of her drink. With clothes in place and hands washed extra well to ward off germs, she softly stepped back into Nick's room, and was greeted by the most beautiful blue eyes staring up at her.

"Shelly!" she cried, stepping out into the hall. "His eyes are open! Nick's eyes are open."

The tears she had been trying so hard to hold back came out with force as she rushed back into Nick's hospital room. Shelly and the on-duty nurse were right behind her, and Charlotte could hear Dr. Rivers being paged over the intercom.

Charlotte stepped up to one side of the bed, with Shelly on the other, as they both waited to see if Nick would look around the room or make any other gesture that he was coming to, but he only had eyes for Charlotte.

"Agent Greyson, my name is Shelly Bert and I'm your patient advocate. If you can hear and understand me, please look my way." Nick continued to look at Charlotte.

"Come around to this side of the bed," Shelly told Charlotte, wanting to see Nick's reaction, and sure enough, his eyes followed Charlotte. Before Shelly had a chance to try anything else, Dr. Rivers rushed into the room and asked for Charlotte to step out. The minute he had the request out of his mouth Nick began to twitch, and Shelly spoke-up.

"Miss Luce seems to be the force that is keeping Agent Greyson calm, Dr. Rivers. It's your call of course, but my professional suggestion is you allow her to stay."

Charlotte mouthed, "Thank you," to her friend, because she had no intention of leaving anyway, but it helped having Shelly behind her. Dr. Rivers nodded his consent and proceeded to look into Nick's eyes and ask him questions. Nick could follow the light, if Charlotte moved with it, but he still wasn't able to communicate, or move his fingers or toes.

At least not for the good doctor. As soon as he was done with his examination and headed out of the room Nick lifted his fore finger and wrapped it around Charlotte's. When his dad and brother came back from grabbing a quick lunch this is how they found them. Starring into each other's eyes, fingers entwined like a lover's bowknot.

Chapter 25
Now

Huge smiles appeared on the faces of Pop and Noah as they stepped closer to Nick's hospital bed. "Is he awake?" Noah asked, "and can he hear us?"

Shelly's smile was genuine as she answered, "I think he's in the process of waking up, but I'm not sure what exactly he hears. It's obvious he knows Charlotte though, and the fact that he moved his finger is another good sign. Coming out of a coma, even a deliberate one, is much harder than it looks on TV, so the best thing we can do is to watch for signs of more comprehension and also signs of stress. The last thing we want to do is put a strain on any part of his body."

Pop moved closer and looked into the face of his namesake, and for the first time since opening his eyes, Nick looked away from Charlotte and up at his father. As much as Charlotte had loved having all his focus, she knew this was a good sign so she gently squeezed Nick's finger. And miracle of miracles, he squeezed back.

"I need to call his mother," Pop told them, his voice cracking as he spoke. "She needs to know that our boy is waking up."

"Do you want me to call her, Pop?" Noah asked, remembering how upset his dad had been when his mother wouldn't come when Nick was first hospitalized.

"No," Pop answered with a shake of his head. "I need to do this myself. You should probably call your sister though, she's going to be upset that she missed all the excitement."

"I'm going to go email both Dr. Rivers and Dr. Copeland about Agent Greyson's progress," Shelly told them. "You'll be okay by yourself, won't you Charlotte? The charge nurse is right next door if you need anything or if there's any more changes; just push the call button and she'll be right here."

Charlotte gave her new friend a nod, but they both knew Shelly was leaving so she and Nick could have a minute alone. Now that he was coming around, her time alone with him would be slim.

For a few seconds, they just looked at each other and then Charlotte lifted the hand she was holding and laid it against her stomach. Pausing to see if there was any recognition of the news she had given him just the day before, Charlotte sat still and waited.

She wasn't sure she could call it a smile but there was a definite change in Nick's mouth. She could see that he was trying to move his lips, so without even thinking she reached over and kissed them. "I've missed you so much, Nick," she murmured, "please hurry back to me. Hurry back to us." The hand laying on her stomach moved slightly, and she realized at that moment, he had not only heard but was acknowledging his child for the very first time.

Chapter 26

Now

Pop wasn't thinking about hospital policy when he pulled out his cell phone to call his ex-wife. All he was thinking about was how thrilled she would be when she heard that Nick was starting to come to. While he waited for her to answer, he couldn't help remembering the night when Nick was born.

"It's a boy!" the doctor had said, laying the screaming baby on his mother's stomach. "Dad, do you want to do the honors?" he had asked Nicholas, pointing to the umbilical cord.

Having a son was most men's dream, but having a healthy child was all that mattered to him. He was totally enthralled with their daughter, Maya, and for him, filling-up the back yard with girls would have been just fine. But it was different for Elizabeth. She had already told her husband that this was going to be her last baby, and now that they had a son and a daughter, their family would be complete.

When Noah came along just one year later Elizabeth Greyson had already decided that life on Anna Maria Island, with a smalltime bait and boat store owner, was not what she had signed on for.

Less than two years later, she packed up her kids and headed home to New York City, looking for big city excitement and leaving behind the man she still loved.

Shelly didn't mean to overhear the conversation, but Mr. Greyson had stopped right outside of her office, and before she could remind him about not using his cell phone inside, she heard his angry words.

"What do you mean you aren't coming to see Nick?" he shouted. "You just told me you were home from your cruise so what else could be more important than being here?"

Shelly stepped back inside, hoping the conversation would end, but the voice she heard was getting louder and more incensed by the minute. She heard the hurt in his voice when he made his final plea.

"Dammit he's our son, Lizzie, he's your son, and he needs to know that his mother still cares."

Shelly had no way of knowing what was said on the other end, but when the phone was pulled from his ear and Mr. Greyson slumped against the wall, it broke her heart.

"Mr. Greyson?" she asked, stepping out of her office. "Is there anything I can do?"

Shaking his head, Nick's father willed himself not to say anything to this lovely young woman that he would regret. "Thank you, Miss Bert, and I apologize for breaking the cell phone rule. I was just so excited to tell Nick's mother that he appears to be coming around that I forgot." He gave her an attempt at a smile so she gave him a caring one in return.

"Well," she said warmly, "I think we can make an exception this one time. Please forgive me if I'm overstepping my bounds, but it doesn't appear that the call went well."

"That's an understatement," he said sarcastically. "I don't know why I even bothered. Nick's mom hasn't shown much of an interest since the day she shipped the kids back to me, but I guess it took this for it to really sink in." He shook his head in disgust and immediately regretted speaking out against his ex-wife.

"I don't know Agent Greyson's mom," she told him, "but things aren't always the way they seem on the outside. What I do know, Mr. Greyson, is that you are a wonderfully caring father, and your family is blessed to have you."

"Thank you, Miss Bert, that's very kind of you to say. And don't you think it's time we dropped the formalities? Most people call me Pop, but my given name is Nicholas."

"Only if you'll call me Shelly, and I think I like Nicholas, it suits you."

Nodding and smiling, Pop walked towards Nick's room with Shelly right beside him.

Chapter 27

Now

Shelly had been right; once the word got out that Nick was coming to, it was rare for Charlotte to be alone with the man she loved. True, Nick was less agitated when she was close by, and he kept his eyes focused on her when she was, but she knew it wasn't fair to his family and friends for her to monopolize his attention. Maya and Dimitri had returned, and several of his friends from the FBI had stopped by as well. There was always a steady stream in and out of his room, at least, when Shelly would allow it.

Charlotte used the time away from him to call both Becca and her mom with updates on Nick's condition, but she kept the news about her pregnancy to herself. She had decided that Nick deserved a voice in how they told their family and friends, so until that time came, her lips were sealed. Shelly was aware of course, but Charlotte knew her secret was safe with her friend the nurse. Not that she thought for a moment Shelly would tell anyone; HIPAA rules didn't allow for the sharing of medical information without permission.

Once Charlotte shared the good news about Nick with her mom, she decided it was the perfect time to ask her about having a guest for an extended visit!

"So, Mom," she said cautiously, "how would you feel about having a visitor?"

"You're coming to visit, Lottie?" her mom asked excitedly. "I didn't think you'd want to leave Nick."

Charlotte took a deep breath, realizing that she hadn't used the right verbiage in her question. "No, not me, Mom, I'm talking about my assistant, Carol Neel. She's out of jail, and the charges have been dropped against her, but she needs a safe place to stay. You're always telling me that your artist commune in Arizona is safer than Fort Knox, and that's what Carol needs. She doesn't really fit the requirements for the witness protection program, but the people her brother worked for may come after her in hopes of keeping him quiet."

When her mother didn't answer right away, Charlotte thought she was going to tell her no, and she was more than surprised when her mom finally spoke.

"You've gone above and beyond for Carol," Maggie said. "I couldn't be prouder of you. I do need to run this past Thomas, but I don't think he'll have any problems with it. When do you think, she'd be arriving?"

"Oh, Mom, thank you so much. I need to talk with her attorney, but I'm sure the sooner the better. Right now, he has her in a safe house of some sort, but he indicated that it was only a short-term arrangement. As soon as you have approval from Thomas, let me know and I'll get information from Owen."

The urge to tell her mom about her impending grandchild was strong, and Charlotte knew she had to end the call. "I need to go now, Mom," she said. "I hope you know I love you, and I appreciate everything you gave up to raise me on your own."

"You're my daughter, Charlotte, the result of the most amazing week of my life, and the blessings you have given me outweigh any sacrifices."

Knowing the tears were coming, Charlotte told her mom once more that she loved her and said goodbye. She had barely ended the call when a text appeared. "Thomas said we'd be happy to have Carol stay with us so just let me know when the plans are made. XOXO."

Breathing a sigh of relief, Charlotte called Owen Gardner with the news and headed back in to see Nick. When she got there, Director James was in his room telling his family that Adam Jennings had been caught and had admitted to shooting Nick. Pop was shaking the director's hand, and Maya was visibly emotional, reliving the details of her brother's assault, but it was Noah who asked the question they all wondered about.

"Why, Director James?" Noah asked with an angry edge to his voice. "After everything he put Stella Harper through, why did he think shooting my brother was going to help him?"

"Obviously, Adam is a troubled young man, and shooting an FBI agent pretty much sealed his fate. From what I understand he got away with stalking Stella for so long that he thought he was invincible. When Nick arrested him, after so many others had failed, he turned his anger and the blame for his own actions towards Nick and vowed that he'd get him one way or another. Thankfully for us, Nick will recover, but Adam's life will never be the same."

Charlotte looked at Nick for a reaction, but his eyes were closed so she hoped he was sleeping. The family walked out with the director and Charlotte followed them, her heart heavy for everything that had happened. Unrequited love had made Adam Jennings do things that were wrong for many years, but he was only twenty-three, and his future looked grim. For many years, she too had thought the love she had for Nick would never be returned, but it had been, and she hoped that her future looked bright.

"Thank you, Gran," Charlotte said with a lump in her throat. "Thank you so much for leading me down the right path and for all the love you and Mom always gave me." Softly caressing her locket, she bowed her head and said a silent prayer for Adam Jennings and whatever he was going to be facing.

Chapter 28
Now

The next morning when Charlotte arrived at Nick's room, she was taken back to find him propped up by pillows, clean shaven with his thick brown hair neatly combed. His voice had been getting stronger each day, but she was not prepared to actually hear him speak.

"Hi," he said in a soft hoarse voice when she entered. For the first time, Charlotte realized she was face to face with the man she had hurt but loved more than anything, and it scared her to death. Communicating with Nick while he was in a coma, or when he couldn't truly respond was one thing, but now he was very much awake and aware of her presence.

"Hi yourself," she responded, not moving any closer to the bed, but it wasn't just Nick's voice that was back. Slowly lifting his hand, he crooked his finger and beckoned her towards him. Tentatively she put one foot in front of the other and moved towards him.

"Sit down," he told her, patting the space on the bed beside him. His voice was still a little shaky, but his intention was not. Charlotte wanted to look away and do anything but look into Nick's eyes, but for some reason she was compelled to do anything but.

As soon as she sat down Nick took her hand in his and without warning said, "So we're going to have a baby." Charlotte tried to pull her hand back away from him, but even after all he'd been through his grip was stronger than hers.

She felt her cheeks heating up but was powerless to stop them or the nausea that was threatening to erupt. *Morning sickness, now?* she asked herself as she willed the queasiness to subside. Taking several short breaths to help her relax, she answered.

"Is that really what you want to talk about, first?" she asked with a little indignation. "I'd like to know how you're feeling, and don't we need to discuss what happened when you came to my house that night?"

"I'll tell you how I feel," he said, his eyes burning deep into her soul. "My body feels like shit, but my heart is lighter than it's been for several weeks, and I always listen to my heart. The woman that I'm in love with is sitting beside me, and she's finally admitted that she loves me in return, and that she's carrying my child. I can't think of anything else we need to talk about, can you? Now come here."

Charlotte couldn't stop the tears from falling as she moved in closer to Nick. She was only prepared for a brief kiss on the lips, but when she got near he pulled her towards him, and the kiss was anything but brief. Thankfully someone had helped him brush his teeth so his breath was minty and fresh, and his lips were firm and demanding.

Trying to get her emotions under control, Charlotte pulled back just enough to stare into his beautiful blue eyes. "Although," he said with a smirk, "I could have done without having Peter and birth control mentioned in the same sentence as when you told me about the baby."

Her eyes as wide as saucers, Charlotte licked her lips before answering. "You heard all that?" she questioned, because she had convinced herself he couldn't have.

"Oh, I heard, all right," Nick said as he tried to reach up to stroke her face. "Luckily for you, and more so for Peter, I wasn't exactly in a position to go all caveman on him."

"So, you're not mad at me, or upset about the baby?" she asked cautiously.

"I never allowed myself to believe we could ever get to this point, but having a child together is more of a gift than I probably deserve. I love you Charlotte Luce, I've loved you for over half of my life, and I promise to love and protect our child with every beat of my heart, for every minute of our life. And now I need to ask you a question that I've wanted to ask for fifteen years." Holding her hand and looking straight into her eyes he asked her, "Lottie, will you be my girl?"

Chapter 29

Now

Shelly came into the room to find Nick and Charlotte wrapped in each other's arms, or as wrapped up as they could be considering Nick was still confined to a hospital bed.

"OK, you two," she said, trying to sound authoritative instead of giddy with happiness about what she saw in front of her. "Your family is clamoring to get in here Agent Greyson, and I don't think I can hold those three big guys off any longer."

Nick gave her one of his warm beautiful smiles and asked, "So you're the amazing Shelly everyone is talking about?"

Shelly wasn't normally one to blush, but the lovely words from the handsome man lying in the bed in front of her caused her cheeks to turn a deep pink.

"Just doing my job, Special Agent, but I have to admit I've grown pretty attached to your family. I can't tell you how happy I am to see how well you're recovering, because your Charlotte is one of my newest friends, and she deserves nothing but the best."

"I couldn't agree more, and please call me Nick. If you're going to be a part of Charlotte's life, we're going to be friends as well."

The words were hardly out of Nick's mouth when his family came rushing in. Pop and Noah had huge smiles on their faces, and Maya had tears running down hers. It was more than obvious how much love was flowing in the room. Even Dimi and the twins were there, although the girls were hiding behind their dad, a little intimidated by all the machines hooked to their beloved uncle.

Charlotte moved away and let Nick talk with his dad and siblings. They had just finished up with the, "How are you feeling," question when Nick spoke up.

"So, what do you think of the news?" he asked beaming.

"What news are you referring to, Son?" Pop asked, with a perplexed look on his face.

"The news about the—" was all he could get out before Charlotte interrupted him.

"The news about Carol Neel being released," she said, trying to get Nick to read her mind. "She's not only been released but the charges against her have been dropped."

"That's wonderful, Lottie," Noah spoke up, "I know how much you care about Carol and believed in her innocence."

Nick looked at Charlotte with confusion but didn't say another word. He wanted to know more about the situation with Carol since that was what had caused their big fight in the first place, but he knew now wasn't the time to address it. He was also confused as to why she stopped him from mentioning the baby, but again, if he had learned anything with Charlotte, it was that timing was everything.

After catching up with all Nick had missed the past two weeks, including the arrest of Adam Jennings, Shelly came in to tell him it was time for him to rest. There were hugs all around, even from Nikki and Stephi, as well as more tears from Maya, but they left without a fuss, just thankful that Nick was awake and alert.

Charlotte bent down to kiss him goodbye, but Nick grabbed her hand and looked deep into her eyes. "Don't go," was all he said, but the pounding in her heart, and the butterflies in her stomach, told her it meant so much more.

Charlotte looked at Shelly for approval and as always was met by her kind-hearted smile. "You can stay a little longer if Agent Greyson promises not to talk and to try to get some rest. The doctors will be in after lunch, and we need him to be fully alert."

"Thank you, Shelly," he said with sincerity, "and it's Nick, remember?"

Shelly nodded and closed the door, leaving Charlotte and Nick alone.

"Why all the secrecy, Charlotte?" he asked her. "Haven't you told my family about the baby?"

"I haven't told anyone, Nick," she responded. "I wanted you to be the first to know. Shelly figured it out before I did, but I haven't told a soul. Not even my mom or Becca and that part's been killing me! But, right now you need to quit talking and try to get some sleep or Shelly will haul my ass out of here."

Nick nodded and grabbed her hand. "I love you, Charlotte." he told her, "and I love that you wanted to share the news with me first. We have a lot to talk about, but I really am tired now so promise me you'll stay for a few more minutes."

"Just try to get rid of me," she answered with a laugh, and then got as comfortable as possible sitting on the side of a hospital bed, holding tightly to the hand of the man she adored.

Chapter 30

Now

By the next morning all the tubes and probes that had been attached to him were gone, and Nick was out of bed and sitting in a chair when his boss, Director James of the Tampa Regional FBI Field Office, stopped by.

"I can't tell you how great it is to see you doing so well," Director James told him. "I've got to be honest and tell you I wasn't sure this story was going to have a happy ending."

Nick nodded at the man who was not only his superior, but also his mentor, and added. "When I opened my front door, and saw Adam Jennings standing there with a gun pointed at me, I had my doubts too. Thankfully he was nervous and not experienced with firearms, or I'm sure the outcome would have been different. What's going to happen to him, anyway?"

"I don't know, Nick, but unless his lawyer is able to prove some kind of mental incapacity, I would say he's looking at spending the rest of his life in prison. Attempted murder of a federal officer is a serious offense."

"Have you spoken with Stella or her mom?" Nick asked, remembering how close he had gotten to the Harper family while he was trying to apprehend Adam for stalking Stella.

"I did talk with Senator Harper, and she conveys her regrets for what happened. I also suggested that it wouldn't be a good idea for either she or Stella to visit you in the hospital, although I know the girl feels terrible about what happened." Director James chuckled before adding. "I've met your Charlotte, and I wasn't sure she'd appreciate having a twenty-one-year-old super model hanging all over you, and we both know that would happen. Stella hasn't matured enough to realize not everything is about her."

Nick let out a big sigh of relief before thanking the director. "Stella doesn't have a mean bone in her body, but she does tend to cause a little drama wherever she goes, and you're right, Charlotte wouldn't understand that at all. We have a lot to talk about, but right now things are looking up, and I don't want anything to get in the way of that."

"So, that brings us to the next issue. Do you have any idea when you'll be getting out of here or able to come back to work? I'm not trying to rush you, just asking."

"I haven't told my family yet, but the doctors say when I can walk down the hall by myself and eat real food, they'll release me. I intend to have both objectives taken care of by tomorrow, so I'm looking at no more than forty-eight hours before I can go home. As for coming back to work," Nick said seriously, "regardless of what the doctors say, I need time to work through some things. "

"I understand," was all Director James said, before shaking Nick's hand and walking towards the door. "And good luck with that beautiful lady of yours, I think she may just be your toughest case ever."

Chapter 31
Now

True to his word, less than forty-eight hours later, Nick was being helped into the living area of his dad's marina, his sister Maya clinging tightly to his elbow.

"You do realize, Mama Bear," Nick laughed, as he used the nickname he and Noah had teased her with when they were kids, "if I go down, you're coming with me? If I fall on you, it won't be pretty."

At almost a foot shorter than her brother, Maya had no intentions of either one of them falling, so she bristled, but kept on walking.

"You listen to me Nicholas Michael," she said in a true Mama Bear tone. "This little escapade of yours took years off my life, so you're going to hold on to my arm and not let go until we reach your bed. Are we clear?"

"Yes ma'am!" he replied, holding tighter to the arm of the sister he loved so much. He really had no interest in going to bed either, but he knew better than to *poke the bear,* so to speak.

Tucked in safe and sound, with a glass of sweet tea and a bowl of soup beside him, the family finally moved out of Nick's bedroom, leaving him alone with Charlotte.

"I feel like I'm a kid again," he complained. "How the hell am I going to recuperate when she's trying to smother me. You have to help me."

Charlotte laughed. "And what can I do? Maya scares the crap out of me, too."

"Come sit with me and see if you can't think of something grown-up we can do? Only for medicinal reasons, of course."

Charlotte walked to the bed and asked coyly, "What do you have in mind?"

Grabbing her by the waist he brought her down until she was snuggled beside him and then took her lips in his. The kiss was raw and electrifying, and when Charlotte pulled back, she could see the desire in his eyes.

"God, I've missed you," he said, pulling her in for another steamy kiss.

Under the sheet, Nick was dressed in a T-shirt and draw string track pants, but there was no hiding his arousal. *Shit, shit, shit,* she thought, surely, he isn't thinking about sex now? Slowly she untangled herself from his arms and moved to the other side of the room.

"Um, I'm not sure what's going on with you right now, but hopefully, you're not thinking I'm going to get naked and get into that bed with you when your family is right outside?"

"I like the naked part a lot, but maybe we can improvise? I need you Charlotte, surely you won't deny a man who just came back from the brink of death?"

His beautiful blue eyes locked on her, Charlotte shook her head. Just the idea that he came back from the brink of death was like stepping into a cold shower, and besides, they needed to talk first, right?

"Come back," Nick pleaded, but Charlotte refused to budge.

Trying a stronger tactic, he said with authority, "Come here," but still, she didn't move.

"Charlotte," Nick said with a growl, but all she did was cross her arms and lift her chin up in the air.

"You can't use your scary FBI voice on me, Nick Greyson," she said defiantly. "I'm an independent woman, not a thug or one of your conquests."

Nick laughed so hard that it pulled on the incision where he'd been shot, making him moan in pain and sending Charlotte to his bedside.

"Are you all right?" she questioned. "Do I need to call your dad? What can I do?"

With the ache in his chest subsiding, Nick stroked her face and said, "You're adorable, Charlotte Luce, but if you think that was my scary FBI voice, you haven't heard anything yet. Now tell me, what's really going on?"

"I'm scared, Nick," she told him honestly, her voice shaky and soft. "I'm scared something is going to happen to you, I'm scared that we don't know each other well enough to bring a baby into the mix. I'm scared I won't be a good mother; I'm scared I won't find a job, and I'm scared that thing," she used her hands to identify the region of his body she was referring to, "is so big it will poke our baby's eye out, or something worse."

Trying not to laugh at her again he grabbed a pillow to hold to his chest, just in case. "That thing?" he asked with mock indignation. "It almost sounds like you're trying to break up with me and I haven't even given you my class ring yet," he teased.

"It's not funny, Nick," she cried. "As much as I want this baby, being pregnant is making me crazy. I'm sick half the time, I'm tired and have to pee constantly, and all of a sudden, my boobs feel swollen and sore, and I don't know what to do. I can't talk to Becca until we decide how to share the news, and Shelly has enough going on at the hospital without mothering me."

"Come here, Lottie," Nick said with love in his eyes, "I didn't mean to make you uncomfortable, and I'm sorry you've had to carry all this on your own. I'm on my way to a total recovery, and I promise you're not alone anymore. I'm sorry that you lost your job, but you'll find another one, I'm sure of it. Now, tell me what the doctor says about your symptoms, and if it's safe for us to make love, because I really feel like I need to comfort those swollen and sore boobs."

Smacking him gently with a pillow, she started to laugh. "*Men!* Is sex all you think about? And I haven't seen the doctor yet, but I have an appointment next week."

"Good, I'll go with you, and we'll find out all the answers together. In the meantime, that thing and I will get to know each other again."

Charlotte gasped, both at the thought of Nick accompanying her to the doctor, and his last remark. Thankfully Maya knocked on the door, giving her an excuse not to respond. Charlotte picked up the bowl of soup and started spoon feeding him. "If you don't eat this we're both in deep shit," she said, but at least for now, her fears were put to rest.

Chapter 32

Now

That night Charlotte was going to sleep in her own bed, and oh, would it feel good! Nick had fallen asleep sometime in mid-afternoon and she had used that as her excuse to leave. As much as she loved the Greyson family, she wasn't used to so much togetherness, and she really needed some time to herself.

Noah drove her home, and while she dreaded being alone with him, she knew they needed to clear the air sometime. As soon as he turned the keys to shut off the engine, she realized that time was now.

"Are we okay, Lottie?" he asked her. "Ever since that morning I came here to see you, I feel as if you're avoiding me, and it's breaking my heart."

More than anything she did not want to hurt his feelings, but how did she tell her good friend that she loved him too, but as a brother and nothing more? Taking a deep breath for courage she began. "It has been awkward, Noah, you're right about that, but with everything happening so fast, I haven't had a moment to think about anything but Nick's recovery. Your friendship has always been precious to me, and I don't want anything to change that, but how do we stay friends after what you said?"

"That I'm in love with you?" he responded. "Those feelings have been there a long time, Lottie, but they didn't affect our friendship before, and they won't now. I'm happy it looks like things are going to work out for you and Nick, but if they hadn't, I wouldn't have tried to step in for myself. I meant it when I said I always knew you were Nick's girl, and I wouldn't have it any other way."

Charlotte smiled, relieved the conversation was out of the way, and her friendship with Noah could continue. She gave him a sisterly kiss on the cheek and stepped out of the car. "Thanks for the ride," she told him, "and for being such a great friend."

Opening the door to her little pink cottage on the beach, Charlotte once again felt the joy that always surrounded her here. Her gran had bought this little bungalow when Charlotte was a baby and had deeded it to her when she graduated from IU. The silver locket she wore around her neck, and this amazing gift, helped her to feel that her grandmother was always close by. "Thank you, Gran," was all she said as she started opening windows to let the Florida sunshine inside.

After airing out her home and making sure everything was okay, Charlotte wanted nothing more than a shower in her own bathroom, and to put on a pair of clean shorts and a T-shirt. Even though she had been able to wash things at Nick's condo, it wasn't the same as having the option of which pair of clean undies to put on.

Her skin glowed after using the Philosophy lemon olive oil scrub she had picked up in the hospital gift shop, and her hair was clean and fresh when she stepped out of the bathroom. Letting the towel drop on her bedroom floor, she looked at herself in the mirror, seeing the visible change in her breasts, and searching for any hint of a baby bump. "I guess it's too soon," she said. "Please remember how hard your mother worked to get this body, kiddo, and don't make me eat for two, thinking I have an excuse."

She had just slathered lotion all over her body when the phone rang. Looking at the caller ID, she saw Nick's name and smiled. "How was your nap?" she asked him.

Nick grumbled. "I'm not five, Charlotte," he told her. "I was resting, not napping. But I miss you, why did you leave?"

Charlotte couldn't help but laugh. "Are you sure about the age thing, because you're sounding a little whiny if you ask me."

"Very funny," was Nick's retort. "But seriously, why did you leave? I've gotten used to having you near-by all the time, and I didn't like waking up and finding you were gone. Were you that upset about earlier?"

"I needed to come home, Nick, it had nothing to do with our conversation," she told him honestly. "I needed a shower and fresh cloths and I can't tell you how much I'm looking forward to sleeping in my own bed. Please understand."

"I do understand, and I'm looking forward to sleeping in your bed, too, but I meant what I said about liking having you close by. Maybe I'm just afraid if I let you out of my sight, I'll lose you again."

"You mean you liked having me close once you came to, right?" Charlotte quizzed.

"No, I could always tell when you were in the room, I just couldn't pull myself out of the darkness to let you know. The way your hair smelled, and the taste of your kiss, made me dream about Hawaii, and us on the beach together. It was a wonderful dream, we have to go there someday."

Charlotte was at a loss for words. "I don't know what to say. Every day I prayed that you knew I was there, I even wore the coconut lip gloss hoping it would bring back a memory, and now you're telling me that it did? That Shelly is one smart cookie!"

"I would eat some cookies if you brought them to me," he said, trying to cajole her, but she held firm.

"I need to stop at Becca's mom's in the morning to pickup my mail, and then I'll be there," she told him firmly. "In the meantime, I'm going to start looking for a job, and your baby and I need a good night's sleep. Now, go let Maya take care of you while she's there, because I promise you, I will not. In fact, once I start cracking my whip you'll be begging for your Mama Bear to rescue you."

"I never thought of you being into that kind of thing, Miss Luce, but you've definitely given me something new to dream about," Nick said, his voice a little huskier than usual.

Charlotte was glad he couldn't see how red her face was, so she decided it was time to end the call. "Good night, Nick, I'll see you tomorrow."

"Charlotte," Nick said softly. "I love you."

Feeling the tears welling up in her eyes, she replied. "I love you, too." Wow. After knowing each other almost twenty years, they had each declared their love to the other, and at the same time! Charlotte grabbed the journal she kept beside her bed and made an entry, hoping they had finally turned the corner for good.

Chapter 33

Now

Old habits die hard, and after a good night's sleep in her own bed, Charlotte was awake by six o'clock, and antsy to get on with her day. Knowing that Maya wasn't leaving until after lunch, Charlotte decided to run down to The Donut Experiment and pick-up a dozen donuts for the Greysons to share. The yummy cake donuts, topped with everything from Key Lime glaze, to maple bacon icing, were one of her weaknesses, but after her firm talk with the baby growing inside of her, she was determined not to eat one.

Slipping on a pair of running shorts and a tank top, she pulled her hair into a messy bun, slipped into her flip flops and then... threw up! "Is this your way of asking for a donut, Babycakes?" she asked as she gracefully tried to get up off the floor. "If you quit doing this to me I promise to give you treats from time to time, okay? But right now, I want to get Daddy a sweet way to start his morning, but I'm going to need some cooperation."

After brushing her teeth for the second time, Charlotte was grabbing her keys when it hit her. Nick was going to be a daddy, and she was going to be a mommy! They had to decide how they were going to tell people, because she needed to talk with Becca, and she needed to talk with her now.

Fresh donuts in hand Charlotte decided she had time to stop and get her mail before going on to the marina. It wasn't quite eight yet, but she knew Mrs. Huddleston was an early riser, too. Ringing the doorbell to Becca's childhood home brought back so many memories. Becca's mom and her house had been a sanctuary for Charlotte a good part of her life, and she had appreciated how loving Mrs. Huddleston had been to her. While some people had snubbed their nose at Maggie Luce and her illegitimate daughter, Becca's mom had always welcomed them both into her home, and Charlotte loved her for that.

"Lottie, it's so good to see you," Mrs. Huddleston said, engulfing her in a big hug. "Becca's been keeping me up to date on Nick, and I have to tell you how thrilled we all are in his recovery. I've had all of the women in my church circle saying their rosaries for him, and it paid off."

The two women spent about thirty minutes catching up until Charlotte had to leave. "I've got donuts in the car for Nick and his family," she said, "and then I have to start looking for a job. Thank you so much for getting my mail every day, it was such a big help."

Mrs. Huddleston was aware of all that had gone on, so she smiled and walked Charlotte to the door. "Come back anytime," she told her daughter's best friend. "Please let me know if there is anything I can do for the Greysons, or for you."

Chapter 34

Now

Pulling into the marina parking lot Charlotte was surprised to see a big, shiny black car already there, and she hoped it meant something good for Pop. She worried his business might have slipped while Nick was in the hospital, so maybe this was a new client with a really big boat that needed to be serviced or stored.

Not wanting to interrupt any business dealings, Charlotte quietly opened the front door of the marina's living quarters, and there in Pop's recliner sat Nick, a long-legged young woman draped across his lap, his arms around her and her face nestled in his neck while she sobbed. An image of the incident at the senior sendoff flashed in front of her eyes, but this time she had the forethought to set the box of donuts down instead of dropping them on the floor.

"Well good morning, Special Agent Greyson," Charlotte said in a rather snarky tone, and then wonder of wonders the young woman jumped off Nick's lap and right into Charlotte's arms. Charlotte caught the look of bemusement on Nick's face, just as the girl started to cry on her shoulder.

"Oh Lottie, I'm so sorry," she cried. "I never thought any of this would happen. Can you ever forgive me?"

Forgive you for what, Charlotte thought. *Snuggling up with my boyfriend or is there more to it than that?* She wanted to go off on the girl but decided to be a grown-up instead.

"Have we met?" Charlotte asked, and as the beautiful face met hers, she knew who the gray eyes filled with tears belonged to.

"I'm Stella, Lottie," she continued to weep. "And we may never have met, but I would have known you anywhere. You're all Nick talked about when he was protecting me from Adam. And he was right, you're so pretty."

Charlotte stole a glance at Nick, and damn if he didn't have the biggest gloat on his face! It was almost as if he was telling her, "Told you so," and that really pissed her off.

Taking a step back, Charlotte looked over the young woman standing before her and reassessed her earlier findings. Stella Harper, this year's *Sports Illustrated* swim suit model and daughter to Florida senator, Linda Harper, wasn't just beautiful, she was stunning. Her black hair billowed down her back and was so shiny Charlotte swore she could see herself in it. Her eyes were a rich dove gray with long feathery lashes, and Charlotte was sure the girl didn't even have on make-up. *Shit, shit, shit,* she thought. *Here I stand in flip flops with my hair up, and to top it all off I probably have a little bit of vomit on my shirt.*

Charlotte was in her own train of thought when she realized that Stella was talking to her. "I never would have thought Adam would go this far," she told Charlotte. "That's why I asked my mom to use her influence to keep him in a minimum-security prison instead of being locked-up with hardened criminals. It's my fault Nick was ever involved and my fault Adam got out." And with that, she started to sob again.

Not at all sure what to do, Charlotte patted the girl's back for a few seconds and then said, "I brought donuts."

Who would have thought a perfect size zero would eat donuts? Of course, that was just another one of the surprises about Stella Harper. She was on donut number two before she even stopped to speak. "Chocolate with sprinkles are my favorite," she squealed, reaching into the box for another one. "How did you know?"

Charlotte didn't have the heart to tell her she hadn't brought the donuts for her, in fact, hadn't even known she would be there, because Stella had finally stopped crying, and Charlotte wanted to keep it that way. About that time, Pop and Noah came in from the deck with a man dressed in a suit, and Charlotte decided he must be Stella's bodyguard, or driver, or both.

The men were drinking coffee and seeing the box of donuts on the table, each helped themselves to one. Charlotte was all about sharing, but to be honest the donuts were for Nick, so while the others moaned about how good they were, she grabbed two of the maple bacon and took them to him.

"Hey," she said with a smile as she handed him the donuts.

"Hey, yourself," he replied, gently pulling her down on his lap. "So, what do you think of Stella?" he asked with a cocky grin. "Is she everything I said she was?"

"Everything and more," Charlotte agreed. "The one thing you didn't mention was that she's one of those people who can eat and not gain weight. I want to hate her for that alone."

Nick laughed and took a bite of donut. "I haven't done much but eat and rest the last few days; will you still love me if I get fat?"

Turning it right back on him, Charlotte asked. "Will you still love me when I get fat?" As soon as the words were out of her mouth she looked to see if anyone had picked up on her slip of the tongue, but thankfully no one had.

Holding his donut in one hand, Nick ran the other one up and down the soft skin of her arm. "I'll love you no matter how much you weigh," he said seriously, "and in my eyes, you'll always be perfect."

For a moment, Charlotte just sat there, thrilled to be hearing the words she had always wanted to hear from a man, but then she couldn't resist teasing him a little bit. "That's the sweetest thing anyone has ever said to me, Nick," she purred. "Here's the thing. I like my men mean and lean, so if you get fat, I can't be held responsible for my actions."

Nick was shocked, and Noah laughed so hard he choked and spit his coffee all over the floor. Charlotte just smiled and leaned down and licked Nick's upper lip. "You had a little frosting right there," she said pointing to his mouth. "I didn't want to see it go to waste, or your waist, whatever the case might be."

Everyone but Nick was laughing at this point, so he grabbed her close and whispered in her ear, "Paybacks are hell, Lottie," and he gave her a full-on, mind blowing kiss… right in front of Stella Harper!

85

Chapter 35
Now

Stella was gone by the time Maya got up around eleven. She came straggling out of her bedroom, dressed in a pair of ratty gym shorts and an old T-shirt, her hair going every which way. "Why didn't someone wake me up?" she asked with a big yawn. Seeing the box of donuts on the table, she helped herself to the last one, accepting a mug of hot coffee from Pop at the same time.

"We thought you could use the rest," her dad told her lovingly. "Between the girls and the restaurant, I don't imagine you ever get to sleep in, and I remember that it's one of your favorite indulgences."

Maya smiled at her dad and looked over at Nick. "Are you going to be okay when I leave?" she asked him. "Someone needs to make sure you take your meds and eat right, but I really need to get home."

"I'm almost thirty-one years old, Maya," Nick reminded her. "I think I can take care of myself. I appreciate everything that you've done for me; I appreciate everything that all of you have done, but it's time for me to take back control of my life, don't you think?"

Charlotte could see tears forming in Maya's eyes, so she stepped in to try to diffuse the tension. "There isn't anyone who can take care of these men like you do, Maya, but I promise I won't let you down. I mean it's not like I have a job to go to, right? So my time is pretty much open."

Charlotte heard Nick groan when she mentioned not having a job, but Pop jumped in to save her. "I need to talk with you about that, Lottie," he said. "Some of the small business owners in the area came to see me last night, because with Tony Neel in jail, we're all out someone to handle our books. I know it's not a fancy job like your one at the bank, but it would sure help us a lot if you would agree to step in, at least until you find something else."

Charlotte was dumbstruck. Her degree was in accounting, and in fact she had graduated from the Kelley School of Business at IU, so she wasn't concerned about being able to do the job and if she could help Pop and his friends out until she got her life figured out, it would at least give her a purpose. Not that taking care of Nick wasn't a purpose, but before long he'd be going back to Tampa and the FBI, and at this moment, she wasn't sure where in that picture she fit.

"It would be an honor to help you out, Pop," she told him with sincerity. "I'm not sure about getting everything from Tony though, I would imagine the FBI confiscated his computer, and what I'll need would be on it."

Nick spoke up. "Let me talk with Director James, and see if Tony used special software, and if so he might agree to letting me have it. If not, I'm sure something can be worked out. It would mean a lot to all of us if someone who knows accounting really goes over Pop's books. Noah and I know just enough to be dangerous, plus, it would mean having you around more."

Charlotte could see the mischief in his eyes, but she liked that he wanted her around more. And with the baby coming, it would be nice to be able to work from home for a while, instead of going into an office. "Okay, I'll do it," she exclaimed, happy that at least for now she could cross one thing off her to-do list.

Everyone was so full of donuts they decided to have a late lunch, and around one Maya packed-up to leave. "When will I see you all again?" she pouted. "We haven't spent this much time together as a family in years, and I kind of liked it."

"Tell you what," Nick said, putting his arm around his sister. "I have a doctor's appointment next week in Tampa, and if Charlotte will agree to be my chauffer, we'll come to Stavros for a family lunch after. I know the girls will be starting school soon, and you and Dimi are busy at the restaurant. It will give us all something to look forward to. Pop and Noah can come too if they want. What do you say?

"I say that sounds wonderful," she told him through her tears, and with a kiss to both brothers, her dad, and Charlotte, she was out the door.

Chapter 36

Now

Charlotte was starving. The whole episode with Stella had foiled her plans of getting at least a piece of toast when she got to the marina, and now her stomach was rumbling and threatening another eruption. She knew the box of donuts was empty, what she didn't know was how to alert Nick to the fact that she needed something in her stomach, and fast!

"You're looking kind of pale, Lottie," Pop told her. "Are you okay? Would you like a cup of coffee or maybe a soft drink?"

The thought of coffee put Charlotte one step closer to bending over the toilet, but a cold carbonated beverage sounded good. "I would love something cold, Pop," she replied. "Coke is fine if you have it."

Slowly moving off Nick's lap, Charlotte accepted the icy cold Coke, along with a plate of cheese and crackers from Pop. "I just realized that you stayed away from the donuts earlier and might need something to eat," he told her with a smile. "Nobody goes hungry on my watch," he boasted, and Charlotte said a little prayer of thanks for this wonderful man in her life.

The snack and the drink were just what Charlotte needed, so when Nick started to yawn, and said he was ready to lie down, she followed him to his room. "Lay down with me," he said, pulling her down on his bed.

They lay there, face to face, for several minutes, and then Nick began to caress and massage her back. "I missed the signs, didn't I?" he asked. "Morning sickness apparently isn't just a morning event."

"Morning, noon, and nighttime, throwing up is an equal opportunity occurrence with this baby," she told him. "Do you think

Pop knows something is up? I mean he's had three kids, so I'm sure he was around when your mom had morning sickness. He's pretty intuitive, you know."

"What do you want to do about telling everyone?" he asked her. "I know it's been hard for you not being able to talk with Becca, so this needs to be your call. Whatever you decide, I'm good with."

Charlotte touched his handsome face and thought again about what to do. She did want to talk with Becca, and her mom would probably be disappointed that she wasn't first on Charlotte's call list, but for right now, she realized she liked this being something special just between the two of them. Besides, they still hadn't talked about what happened with Carol, or where this relationship was headed, and maybe all that needed to be worked out first.

"Why don't we wait to decide until after my doctor's appointment on Monday? I need to know everything is okay before telling anyone else, and it will give us time to talk about what happened a few weeks ago, as well as, what's going to happen next. Is that fine with you?"

Charlotte saw the fear in his eyes, not only concern for their baby, but for the conversation she wanted to have about his investigation of the Neels. When he pulled her in for a kiss she laughed inwardly, knowing he was diffusing the conversation in a way only a man knows how to. By the time she came up for air, her hormones were raging, and all thoughts of talking were lost.

Nuzzling her neck, Nick told her, "How about we make a decision after both our appointments next week? By then we'll have talked with the doctor about our baby, and I'll have a better handle on when I can return to work. My appointment is on Thursday so it works out perfectly. We can talk on our way back from Tarpon Springs and put a plan in place."

Charlotte nodded her agreement and then blurted out, "I've been calling it Babycakes, is that a problem for you?"

"So, you want a girl?" Nick asked her.

"I never thought about it," Charlotte responded honestly. "I was talking to it this morning, and well it's a baby, and I really love the cake donuts from the Donut Experiment so it just kind of happened. Becca has both varieties of kids, and I love them equally, so honestly I don't care, do you?"

"I love you," Nick told her. "I don't care if it's a girl or a boy if you're happy." Nick's declaration was filled with such a sense of support and commitment that Charlotte couldn't help but melt a little.

She looked up at Nick with pure devotion. "I am happy Nick, I really am," she said. "I can't wait to know that our baby is healthy, and that we can, you know, be together again."

"That makes two of us," was all he answered, and he closed his eyes and rested, because naps were for kids!

Chapter 37
Now

The rest of the weekend went well, and before she knew it, Monday morning was here, and it was time for her first OB appointment. After several weeks of wearing the same thing, or throwing on shorts and a tank top, Charlotte was happy to finally get dressed up. Deciding on turquoise ankle length pants, and a white silk T-shirt, strappy sandals, and sea glass earrings, she put on the locket from her gran, and looked in the mirror. Not exactly market president attire, but not bad for an unwed mother, she told herself. "Oh Gran, where did I go wrong?" she silently asked her grandmother. "The last thing in the world I ever wanted to do was follow in my mother's footsteps, and that's just what I've done."

By the time she arrived at the marina to pick Nick up, she was edgy and nervous, and nothing he said could calm Charlotte down. "You really need a woman to talk to, don't you?" he asked her.

"I could have called Shelly; I should have called Shelly, but I had no idea I'd have these feelings. Becca's who I really need right now, but we agreed to wait, and that's what I'm going to do. But oh Nick, what if something is wrong with our baby? Or if there's a problem with me, I just don't think I could take it."

Nick let out a deep breath before answering. "I can't begin to understand what you're going through, but I truthfully believe that everything is okay with both of you. You're young and healthy, you eat right and exercise, and babies are born every day to women with a lot less going for them than you have. But, never forget this. No matter what we find out today, or what happens in the next seven and a half months, we're in this together, and that's not something you ever need to doubt."

How could such simple words turn her world inside out? "Thank you, Nick. Just hearing that, and knowing you mean it, may keep me from going over the edge," she said softly. "I guess it's still hard for me to believe this is all really happening."

"Oh, it's happening," he chuckled, "and I know how incredibly fortunate I am to be a part of it. You and Babycakes are my everything."

The drive to Bradenton went by quickly and soon Charlotte and Nick were seated in the waiting room of a large OBGYN practice. Pregnant women, nursing mothers, and young children filled the room, and Charlotte felt another wave of panic start to overtake her. She was reaching for her locket, to have a heart to heart with her gran, when Nick put his arm around her.

"Relax, Charlotte," he said firmly. "Relax and just breathe."

Charlotte nodded and started in on the paperwork the receptionist had given her. When she came to the part about her insurance carrier Nick swore. "Shit," he said quietly, "I didn't even stop to think about insurance now that you're not working. I'm pretty certain I can get the baby on mine but…"

"Now it's your turn to relax, Nick. The bank agreed to keep me on their insurance until my severance package runs out, and then I'll be covered by COBRA for eighteen months. One way or another, my medical will be covered and so will the baby's."

"I feel like such an ass," he said, shaking his head. "I want to take care of you, but you keep taking care of me."

"Maybe we can take care of each other," Charlotte told him with a smile, and Nick agreed.

"Maybe we can."

When Charlotte's name was called to go in to see the doctor she realized that she was a little uncomfortable with the thought of Nick being there while she was examined. "You don't have to go in with me," she told him sweetly. "I promise I'll tell you all that I find out."

"No dice, Lady," he said with authority. "I want to see and hear everything for myself."

Trying her feminine powers of persuasion, she asked him, "Do you really want to see me naked on a table with a strange man looking up my hoo ha?"

"You naked on a table conjures up all kinds of erotic thoughts," he smirked, "but it's a medical examination, Charlotte, and it isn't going to be a problem."

She was trying to come up with a response to sway Nick to her way of thinking when the nurse once more said her name and held the door wide open, as if to say, "Get in here, now." Nick gave the nurse a wink and a smile, and Charlotte saw the woman blush. *Brother! Why is it a man can get by with almost anything when he's tall, dark, and handsome?* she thought.

Chapter 38

Now

At the nurse's insistence Charlotte stepped up on the scale and was pleased to see she had lost five pounds. *Evidently there is an upside to morning sickness after all,* she thought, even though she knew for her baby's sake losing weight was not the goal right now. Her blood pressure and heart rate were both recorded, and the nurse handed her a cotton hospital gown and a sheet and told her to put the gown on, open to the front, and sit up on the table. *Crap! Can this be anymore humiliating?* Charlotte thought.

Seeing the humor in Nick's eyes, she told him sternly, "Close those baby blues and don't even try to peek. I'll let you know when it's okay to open them."

Charlotte wasn't quite sure why this bothered her so much, after all, he had seen pretty much every inch of her body unclothed, but this wasn't the same, and she was embarrassed. Horribly embarrassed.

Seated on the examination table, the gown held as securely closed as possible, and the sheet wrapped tightly around her legs, Charlotte was trying to get up the nerve to look Nick's way, when there was a knock on the door, and the doctor walked in.

"Mrs. Luce, Mr. Luce, I'm Dr. Mark Stanley," he said, shaking Nick's hand, and Holy Crap! He was tall, gorgeous, and young!

Charlotte could see the color creep up on Nick's face, because the doctor looked a lot like his brother Noah. Charlotte didn't know if Nick was aware of Noah's profession of love to her or not, but the look on his face made her believe that he was. "Um, actually it's Miss Luce, but please call me Charlotte," she said, trying to get the attention off of her hot new doctor, "and this is—"

"Nick Greyson," Nick said forcefully, "I'm the baby's father."

"Well, Charlotte, Mr. Greyson—"

"Special Agent Greyson," Nick corrected him, and OMG, Charlotte was mortified! She had never seen Nick posturing like this, and the thought of it made her giggle like a school girl. She could see his hands were clenched in tight fists, and she was scared to death he was going to ask the doctor to step outside! Men!

"Again, Charlotte, Special Agent Greyson," Dr. Stanley started, with an emphasis on Agent. "It's very nice to meet you both, so now let's focus on your baby and your health."

Charlotte breathed a sigh of relief to be moving on and was thankful to be able to ask about her morning sickness, as well as what she should expect in the next few months. That part of the visit over, the doctor asked her to scoot back on the table and put her feet in the stirrups so he could feel her uterus. Charlotte knew her face was beet red lying like this, with Nick in a chair across the room. When she looked at him, his face was also beet red, probably because the young doctor had his hand up inside of her. *I tried to tell you*, she thought.

"Everything looks great," Dr. Stanley told them. "Everything is right where it should be at roughly two months into your pregnancy, and your blood pressure and weight are excellent, although I do want you to start on prenatal vitamins and to take them throughout your pregnancy. They may not settle right since you're experiencing morning sickness, so take them with toast, or something dry and easy on your stomach, until that passes. Do you have any questions?"

"Is there anything I shouldn't do?" Charlotte asked him. "I usually run several times a week; is that something I have to stop?"

"Absolutely not," Dr. Stanley answered. "You can continue any activity you do now, unless of course it causes you discomfort. If that's all then I'll send you out to pick up your vitamins and to set up your next appointment. We'll do an ultrasound at that appointment too, so plan to be here a little longer. After that, I'll see you every month until closer to your due date, but if you have any problems don't hesitate to call and we'll get you right in." The doctor stood up and shook

Charlotte's hand and was just about to the door when she heard Nick clear his throat.

Shit! Shit! Shit! She was really going to have to do this. "Um, Dr. Stanley, I do have another question," Charlotte said, trying to avoid looking at either man. "How about sex? Is it safe for the baby?"

Dr. Stanley smiled and looked at Nick and then at Charlotte. "It's perfectly fine," he told them both. "In fact, it's a good stress reliever for you and won't hurt the baby at all. Of course, just like with your running, if you have any discomfort or bleeding, call the office right away. But for the most part, I'm going to tell you that your baby is well protected in a snug little cocoon, and you don't need to worry that something you do in the normal course of life is going to hurt it."

The doctor left the room and Charlotte got dressed as quickly as possible, doing her best not to look Nick's way. Neither one of them spoke to the other, and the tension between them was so sharp that when they went back to the waiting room, she was sure everyone in the office could feel it.

Nick put his hand on her back and ushered her out of the building—after appointments had been made and a big bottle of prenatal vitamins was safely in her purse—but Charlotte wasn't feeling any comfort from it. Normally his touch made her feel warm and tingly, but this felt more like a father leading an errant child.

Since Charlotte was driving, Nick led her to her car door and then settled himself in the passenger's seat. She sat there for a moment, but instead of starting the car she looked his way and asked, "What's your problem, Nick? I warned you this appointment might be uncomfortable."

She could see he was struggling to put his thoughts into words, but she just sat there, refusing to make it any easier on him. Finally, he spoke. "I thought the doctors who delivered babies were old men, you know, like a grandfather. I certainly didn't expect to see some kid touching and looking at you in places only I should be able to look at and touch. I felt like I was in the middle of a porn movie, and for heaven's sake, Charlotte, he was about twelve!"

Charlotte turned her head because she was about to laugh out loud, and she knew that wouldn't help the situation. Once she got her emotions under control, she reached over and touched his hand and smiled. "Are you jealous, Nick? Because it is one thing I never expected from you."

"You're damn right I'm jealous," he spat at her. "You're my woman, and no one gets to touch you but me." Charlotte continued to smile and all of a sudden he said, "Did that sound as bad to you as it did to me?"

Charlotte nodded and leaned over and gave him a soft, sweet kiss. "I kind of love that you're jealous," she told him, "but he's a doctor, Nick, and a good one. He doesn't even take new patients but Shelly was able to get me in. And hopefully, he won't let the whole *He Man* routine keep him from continuing to see me. You want the best care for us, right?"

Nick nodded and smiled back at her. "I kind of made a fool out of myself, didn't I?" he said. "I can't believe that I acted like such a girl!"

"Let me remind you Special *Agent* Greyson," Charlotte said, emphasizing the agent like Dr. Stanley did, "if you were a girl, I wouldn't be in this condition now, would I?" Nick shook his head and laughed, and she laughed right along with him.

"Although," she added, just wanting to keep him on his toes, "he is awfully pretty!" Nick growled and Charlotte grinned. Charlotte one, Nick zero!

Chapter 39

Now

By the time they arrived back at the marina they found Pop setting out a lunch fit for a king, or in this case eight of them, because gathered around the table were eight of the area's small business owners who Charlotte had agreed to work for. She knew Nick was hoping they could have some one on one time, now that they had the official green light from her doctor, but she needed this job and there was no way she was going to let down these men who were counting on her.

Charlotte saw the frustration on Nick's face and knew she needed to take control of the situation before he had another meltdown. She made a mental note to ask Shelly if any of the meds he was on could be causing him side effects. The last thing she needed was two babies to take care of, especially not one who was a head taller and probably eighty pounds heavier than she was.

"Gentlemen," Charlotte addressed the group assembled around the table. "What a nice surprise it is to be able to meet you all at once and for us to have lunch together. I know I'm starving. Why don't we relax and eat this yummy spread Pop put together, and then we can talk business?"

Without waiting for them to agree, Charlotte took Nick's arm and led him to the table and the seat next to hers. *Don't mother him*, she told herself, as she started to assemble herself a sandwich, and *please Babycakes, let me keep this food down!*

To her delight the sandwich and fresh fruit stayed put and didn't even cause any queasiness. The conversation was mainly directed at Nick, with questions about Tony Neel, the security of their personal information, and of course his being shot by the man he had captured who had stalked Stella Harper for over a year. Charlotte was happy to see Nick relax and enjoy himself, but it didn't take long for her to see he was starting to drag.

Everyone helped Pop clear the table and Charlotte took that opportunity to get Nick alone. "We've had a really busy morning," she told him, "and I can see how tired you look. Why don't you go rest while I get some information from the guys, and then later we can go for a walk on the beach. Babycakes and I need you," she said softly, hoping to prevail upon his sense of duty. "You need to take care of yourself if you're going to take care of us."

She had expected him to argue, but instead he nodded in agreement. "I am tired," Nick admitted. "I wish you could come lie down with me, but I know how important it is to you to be working." He started to head to his room but turned around and pulled her into one of his mind-blowing kisses. When he stepped away, Charlotte was weak kneed and couldn't think of a single reason why she was going back into a room of middle-aged men when she could be snuggled in the arms of a young and very delicious one.

Chapter 40

Now

Everything hurt. After sitting on a kitchen chair, hunched over the kitchen table for hours on end, Charlotte was exhausted. She vaguely remembered seeing Nick emerge from his bedroom, and sit down in Pop's recliner, and hearing the pizza deliveryman at the door. Every other possible minute was spent getting information from the group of men sitting around her.

She knew at some point she wolfed down a piece of cheese pizza and guzzled down at least two real cokes, and thankfully nothing had tried to come back up. Her hand was cramping, and her eyes were crossing when she felt warm strong hands massaging her neck. And oh, they felt good.

"Guys," Nick started in, "it's time for me to take Charlotte home. She's had a long day and needs some sleep."

Charlotte started to protest, and so did the group of business owners, but Nick wasn't having any of it. "I'm taking you home now, Charlotte," he said forcefully, and she nodded, thankful her strong G-man was back!

After arranging some individual appointments with the men and thanking Pop for organizing everything, Charlotte grabbed her purse and her keys and started for the door.

"Keys?" was all Nick said to her, and she was both embarrassed and thrilled.

"You're not supposed to drive yet," she reminded him, but that didn't stop him from taking the keys out of her hand.

"Your house is only a few miles away," Nick told her, "and you can hardly keep your eyes open. At this point, I think it's safer for me to drive than for you." Charlotte didn't want to give in, but she knew he was right, so reluctantly she followed him to her car.

It felt so good to be home! Nick fixed her a glass of water and told her to get ready for bed, and for a moment she was a little worried about what he had in mind. Surely he wasn't thinking about sex now, was he? She was dead on her feet and needed a shower, but she was just too tired to take one.

After running a warm rag over her face, Charlotte put on her IU sleepshirt, hoping Nick would get the hint. When she walked back into her bedroom she saw he had turned back the covers and was waiting for her by the bed.

Shit! Shit! Shit! she thought. I don't even have the strength to argue with him. Maybe I can just lay there and let him do his thing?

Charlotte stood there as Nick brushed a lock of strawberry blond hair out of her eyes and took her face in his hands. "You couldn't be any sexier if you were wearing black lace," he told her, his voice a little huskier than normal, "but I can wait for that time, because you need to sleep." She was so grateful that she allowed him to help her into bed, and even tuck her in.

The minute her head hit the pillow Charlotte felt her eyes close as big strong hands rubbed up and down her weary spine. She was lost somewhere between heaven and earth when Nick's hand moved slowly around to her stomach and started lightly caressing it. She was almost on the verge of reminding him that she was too tired for romance when she heard him softly say, "Good night Babycakes," and when she drifted off to sleep, all of her dreams were sweet.

Chapter 41

Now

Charlotte woke-up, confused at first at the feeling of being unable to move, but glancing behind her, she saw the object of her immobility sleeping soundly, his large leg covering hers, while his arm was tightly wrapped around her waist. She smiled at how normal it felt falling asleep with Nick beside her, but as she carefully wiggled away from his hold, she realized he was still dressed in his T-shirt and shorts from the day before. Well, maybe normal was taking it a little far, she thought, but it had at least been comfortable!

The clock on her phone said it was eight and Charlotte knew she needed to get a move on it to make it to the first appointment with her new independent business owners group. Quietly padding into the kitchen, she put a pod of Emeril's dark roast in her Keurig for Nick and poured him a big glass of the fresh orange juice she had picked up at Mixon's Fruit Farm. By the time she returned to her bedroom, Nick was just opening his eyes, and he reached for her as she sat down on the bed.

"How did you sleep?" was the first question out of his mouth. Handing him the glass of juice, Charlotte admitted that she hadn't slept so well in weeks. When Nick reached for the mug of coffee Charlotte let out a little wistful moan at how good it smelled.

"You aren't having any?" he asked, knowing that coffee was one of her favorite morning rituals.

"I haven't had any since Shelly told me I was pregnant," Charlotte said with a smile. "For the last few weeks, just the smell of it was enough to make me nauseated, but I have to admit that I miss it. I'm feeling pretty good this morning though, so maybe my morning sickness is a thing of the past."

Nick held his mug up to her and offered to share. "Well, maybe just one sip," she said eagerly. The first sip was like ambrosia, so she took a second and a third and then…! Shoving the coffee mug into Nick's hands, Charlotte ran to the bathroom, barely getting the door shut and locked before the coffee came right back up.

Nick was on her heels, but she refused to let him in the bathroom with her. "Charlotte," he demanded, "open the door."

Her stomach empty and her dignity bruised, Charlotte curled up on the bathmat and tried to will herself to disappear.

"I'm serious, Charlotte," Nick told her as he pounded on the door. "Let me in right now."

But she held firm. Throwing up was never meant to be a team sport, and she wasn't about to make it one now. The problem was she had to get showered and dressed for her appointment, but her stomach was still hovering on the side of queasy. She wanted Nick to go away so she could vomit and shower in peace, but when he changed his tactics, she knew she had lost the battle.

"Charlotte, please," Nick pleaded, but it was the concern she heard in his voice that got her. "Honey, I'm worried about you, please open the door and let me in."

Did he just call me, Honey? Scooting over to the door she turned the lock and lay back down on the rug. Nick was one big guy, but the look of helplessness on his face was enough to make her smile.

"Are you still sick?" he asked cautiously. "Are you ready to get up?"

Deciding Babycakes had put on enough of a show for one morning, Charlotte got up and let Nick lead her back to bed. "Do you have crackers?" he asked her. Once her pillows were propped and her color was coming back to normal, Nick left Charlotte in search of something bland.

"I found a box of saltines" he told her when he returned, handing her a stack of the dry, salty crackers. "Eat a few before you try to get back up and see if they help."

Still a little embarrassed by the whole throwing up thing, Charlotte nibbled on the crackers and tried not to make eye contact with Nick. She wasn't used to having someone coddle her, and as nice as it was, she felt uncomfortable being treated as an invalid. She was just about to thank him and explain her feelings when he looked her in the eye and said, "I'm so sorry, Lottie."

She let the Lottie go, but did wonder what he was sorry about. "Why are you sorry, Nick?" she questioned. Had he changed his mind about wanting the baby?

"I'm sorry that you're so sick," he said softly. "I'm not sorry that you're pregnant," he told her honestly, "because I already love this baby, but I am sorry that being pregnant is so rough on you. Will it always be this way, because I'd like to have a whole houseful of kids?"

Hold the freakin phone! A whole houseful of kids? They hadn't even discussed the future, heck they still needed to talk about what had happened with Carol and the FBI sting, and he was already thinking about more babies?

"It's not your fault that I'm having morning sickness, Nick," she told him "Although you did knock me up." Seeing the horror in his eyes she laughed to let him know she was just pulling his chain. "And as far as other kids, how about we just enjoy this one for now, and see where things go from there?"

Nick nodded and gave her a chaste kiss on the cheek. "You have your first meeting in forty-five minutes," he told her. "I'm going to go fix you one of the English muffins I saw in your fridge while you shower and get dressed. You don't want to be late for your first day on the job."

Charlotte smiled and nodded as she carefully got out of bed. *He loves our baby*, she thought as she turned on the water of the shower, and just knowing that was worth every day of morning sickness she would endure.

Chapter 42
Now

After a healthy, but light, breakfast of a perfectly toasted English muffin and a cup of yogurt, Charlotte was revived and ready to start her day. Nick wanted to get home so he could shower and change clothes, plus he told her, there was real breakfast food at the marina. He was on the verge of telling her his mouth was watering for a big plate of bacon and eggs, but after the coffee incident earlier, he decided mentioning greasy food might not be a good idea.

"When will I see you again?" he asked as she pulled into the marina parking lot.

"After the appointment at the Galleria with Mr. Stevens I need to go home and make some calls. I haven't talked to my mom or Becca in days, and I'm sure they're both ready for an update. After lunch I have an appointment at The Book Nook with the Wells, and then I'll swing by."

"Swing by?" he asked, looking dejected. "Does that mean you aren't going to stay?"

Shit! Shit! Shit! She had to ask Shelly about those meds! She didn't know how to cope with Nick's mood swings, but not wanting to upset him she answered. "Of course, I'll stay, at least for a while, but I don't want Pop feeling as if he's adopted another child. Maybe we can take him out for dinner and we'll see how the evening goes, okay?"

"I think he adopted you a long time ago," Nick responded, "but I agree, it would be nice to get him out of the marina for dinner." Giving her hand a kiss, Nick opened the car door and stepped out. "I love you, Charlotte," he told her, and then she watched him walk away.

Rolling down her window as she sped off, Charlotte yelled out. "I love you, too!" Nick turned around and graced her with one of his megawatt smiles.

The meeting with Clay Stevens went well, and Charlotte started to feel better about her new position. Clay was only about ten years older than she was and had kept great records, despite having Tony Neel handle his official books. A transplant from Atlanta, Clay was an attractive man who Charlotte had seen over the years around town, but she had never given him much thought otherwise.

"So," Clay said to her as she was getting up to leave, "are you and Nicolaus Greyson's son an item, or are you just friends?"

Shit! Shit! Shit! she thought. Was Clay Stevens hitting on her?

Putting on her most professional smile she answered him. "I guess saying we're an item is as good a term as any. We've known each other since we were kids and had reconnected before his accident." And I'm carrying his baby, she wanted to say, and other than that our relationship hasn't been totally defined. But of course, she didn't!

Clay seemed to understand, and she told him she would be in touch, but the elephant in the room made it hard for her to breathe. She knew this was not something she could share with Nick. She left the Galleria, stopped at the health food store for a salad, and headed home to call Becca. This was just one of those times when only a girlfriend would do!

Chapter 43

Now

The call to Becca was just what Charlotte needed, although it was killing her not to be able to tell her friend she was pregnant. It was especially hard because Becca was pregnant as well, and Charlotte knew how fun it would be for them to experience this special time together. Just a couple more days, she told herself, and then Nick and I can talk and decide how to share the news about Babycakes.

As much as she had dreaded the call to her mom, it went surprisingly well, and Charlotte was thrilled to hear Carol was acclimating to her new life in Arizona. Owen Gardner had told Charlotte that for Carol's protection, and the safety of her mom and Thomas, they needed to be careful discussing the situation by phone or text, so she, Charlotte, and Maggie had come up with a code!

"The kitty is doing so well in our home," Maggie told her daughter, "and both Thomas and I love her. So far, we've been really careful about letting her out on her own, but some of the others in the artist colony have taken a shine to her and promised to keep an eye on her if she gets out."

Charlotte smiled, thinking of her friend Carol being referred to as a cat, but she understood the importance of keeping her location a secret and went along with it. She hoped that Carol was happy and that they would be able to see each other sometime soon.

"How are the wedding plans coming, Mom?" Charlotte asked. "I hope having a new pet in the house isn't affecting them?"

"Nonsense, Lottie," Maggie replied. "Thomas and I are getting married as soon as his son, Chad, can get here, and that should still be in October or November at the latest. You're still coming, aren't you? The situation with Nick won't make you change your mind?"

Charlotte knew her mom hadn't been a fan of Nick's ever since she had told her what happened at the senior sendoff, but lately she seemed a little more resigned to him being back in her daughter's life. *Wait until I tell her Nick and I are expecting a baby*, Charlotte thought.

"I'll still be there, Mom," Charlotte reassured her mother. "Nothing could keep me away, but I hope that you'll be okay if Nick comes with me? I haven't asked him yet, and I don't know if he'll even be able to come, but I want you to be comfortable with him, if it works out."

"You're a grown woman, Charlotte Louise, and you don't need your mother's approval on the man in your life. If Nick Greyson is who you want, you know I'll support you."

"He is, Mom," Charlotte replied softly. "He's all I've ever wanted."

The call ended and Charlotte realized it was almost time for her appointment with Geoff and Lydia Wells at The Book Nook. Grabbing her purse and her keys Charlotte set off with a smile on her face. Not only was The Book Nook one of her favorite places on the island, she'd talked with Becca and her mom and kept her lunch down! It was going to be a great afternoon.

Chapter 44

Then

Lottie had always been an avid reader, even though math and numbers were her first love. From the time they were old enough to walk to town on their own, she and Becca had spent many a Saturday morning at The Book Nook, looking over the newest mystery novels, and deciding on which ones were worthy of their money. Even after she had decided she was being called to be a nun, Becca had loved a good mystery, so the girls always bought books they could share back and forth.

The chimes on the front door of the book shop were almost as welcoming as the bell at Two Scoops, and Lottie loved each place equally. Stepping into a world of books was like stepping into a world of dreams, and Lottie had plenty of those.

"Well, Good Morning, Lottie," Mrs. Wells said to her from the wonderful old desk where she sat. "And where is the other half of the Hardy Girls this morning," she teased. Lottie blushed, but was secretly pleased that Mrs. Wells didn't mind the time she and Becca spent browsing through the shelves.

"Becca had something going on at church today," she answered the kind shop keeper. "I knew that you were getting new books in this week, and I just couldn't wait!" Lottie looked up at the smiling woman before her and thought, *She's so beautiful, I hope I look just like her when I grow up.*

After looking over all the new arrivals, Lottie gingerly picked up the latest book in the Harry Potter series and gave it to Mrs. Wells to ring up. Gran had sent her some money in a valentine, and Lottie had been saving it for something special. If a new *Harry Potter* book wasn't special, what was?

"No coffee today, Lottie?" Mrs. Wells asked her. The Book Nook served free coffee to its patrons, and despite their young age, Mrs. Wells always offered the girls a cup with lots and lots of cream! As she grew older. Charlotte often wondered if that's where her love of coffee began.

"Thank you very much," she replied, remembering to be polite, "but I told my mom I wouldn't be gone long, so I'd better head back home." Taking her treasured package in her hand, Lottie smiled again at Mrs. Wells, and ran home, anxious to see what Harry was up to this time!

Chapter 45

Now

Stepping in to The Book Nook, was like stepping back in to her childhood. Everything looked the same and smelled the same, and Mrs. Wells was still seated at the big oak desk in the front, just as she had been the last time Charlotte was here. Memories were about to overcome her when Mrs. Wells spoke.

"Well, Lottie Luce," she said with a grin. "It's like old times having you here in the shop. There aren't any new *Harry Potter* books for you to read, but I do have a pot of fresh coffee?"

Charlotte looked at the woman standing before her and was amazed that she hadn't changed any more than the bookstore had. "Mrs. Wells you look just like you did when I was a little girl!" Charlotte exclaimed. "I used to think you were so beautiful, and I wanted to be just like you. And the shop's just the same, how in the world did I forget about what a wonderful place this is?"

"I imagine when you left for college you didn't have a lot of time to read for pleasure, am I right? And at some point, you probably got an eReader, and left the world of bound books behind."

Charlotte was embarrassed, because the woman was right. She had forgotten the wonders of holding a real book in her hand, but she knew that was about to change. "I need to pass on the coffee," she said, "but I am ready to step back into the world of real books, and not just the electronic kind. We can get started looking over your books, no pun intended, or I can shop and then we'll work. It's up to you, Mrs. Wells."

"You're all grown-up now, Lottie, so please, call me Lydia." Mrs. Wells told her. "And are you sure about the coffee?"

Charlotte nodded, knowing she couldn't risk another episode like she'd had that morning. "You're right, Lydia, I am all grown-up, and I would love it if you would call me Charlotte."

And with that the two women hugged and spent a few minutes catching up before Lydia's husband Geoff came out of the back office. After deciding to work on the financial books first, Charlotte followed Geoff to his office but promised Lydia she would be back to shop before she left.

Just as with Clay Stevens, the Wells kept good records, so Charlotte was able to complete her assessment much faster than she had thought. She didn't want to put herself out of a job, but she was curious as to why these independent business owners were paying for accounting services when they seemed to be on top of things on their own.

"I don't want to look a gift horse in the mouth," Charlotte began, "because this job truly is a gift, but I have to ask why you were paying Tony Neel, and why you're willing to pay me, when you keep such complete records yourself?"

Lydia stepped into the office with a cup of fresh coffee for her husband. "I can answer that," she offered. "Geoff and I do like to know where we stand financially, which is why we kept a copy of everything that we sent Tony, but we like to travel when we can, and sometimes that means being gone when bills need to be paid, or worse yet, taxes. We decided about five years ago that instead of selling the shop and totally retiring, we'd do a semi-retire and work when we want, and still be able to do other things. We hired a store manager who works three days a week, plus takes over when we're away, but it didn't seem right to ask her to handle the books as well."

Charlotte nodded, understanding and admiring what Lydia was telling her. How great it must be to be to work alongside of your partner, be your own boss, and be able to do the things in life you love. If this job worked out for her, she was at least a third of the way there, right?

After gathering what she needed from Geoff's office, Charlotte went back into the book shop on the hunt for a book for Nick. She had a feeling he was probably starting to go a little stir crazy just taking it easy every day, so hopefully a good book would be just the thing.

"What can you recommend for my friend, Nick Greyson?" Charlotte asked Lydia Wells.

"Your friend?" Lydia teased her. "When Geoff came home from the meeting at the marina on Monday, he told me how protective Nick was of you; maybe friend isn't quite the right word?"

Charlotte was trying hard not to blush, but damn if she didn't anyway! "You're right, we are more than friends, but I'm still looking for just the right definition. Maybe what I need is a Thesaurus?" she teased back.

"I'm sure you'll work out all the details on your own," Lydia told her, "but we are happy for both of you. Geoff and I remember how inseparable you and Nick were when you were younger, and we always wondered what made that change. Anyway, let's get a book for that man of yours."

What made that change? Charlotte thought. *A self-centered hussy by the name of Ashley, and a self-conscious coward, by the name of Lottie.*

Changing the subject as quickly as possible, Charlotte asked for a book recommendation for Nick. "There's a new Michael Connelly out," Lydia said taking Charlotte to the mystery section. "Do you know if he's read any of the Harry Bosch books? Harry's a police detective in Los Angeles, and Geoff and I both love the series'"

Charlotte shook her head. "I really don't know what he's read, but it sounds like something he'd like. Is there a beginning to the series that maybe I should start out with?"

"*The Black Echo* is the first in the series and was also Connelly's debut novel. It was written in ninety-two, so it's been around awhile, but it's a great starting place. I'll tell you what. Why don't you take *The Black Echo* and the second book, *The Black Ice*, and see what Nick thinks. If he's read them you can bring them back and we'll find something else. And there's no charge, by the way"

"That's so kind of you, Lydia, but are you sure?" Charlotte asked.

"Absolutely," Lydia replied. "I'd do anything to help Nick Greyson. If he hadn't stopped Tony Neel, there's no telling what might have happened to any of us who allowed Tony to have access to our funds. From what the FBI director told us, Tony was already starting to kite checks between the accounts he handled, but thankfully none of us had lost anything yet."

Charlotte felt so ashamed. She had never thought of what Tony Neel was doing to the people who trusted him with their finances. All this time, she had blamed Nick and the FBI for what had happened to Carol, and ultimately to her, when the real culprit was Tony Neel.

Charlotte left The Book Nook with the package for Nick, and a whole new perspective on the sting against Tony Neel. Yes, she wished Nick would have confided in her about what was going on, but as much as she hated the entire situation, she understood now how important it had been. She knew she needed to make amends to him for the way she had acted.

Chapter 46

Now

Pop was on the dock talking with a customer, and Nick was hunched over his laptop when Charlotte returned to the marina. Being as quiet as possible to surprise him, Charlotte wrapped her arms around his neck and whispered in his ear, "Hey handsome, whatcha' reading?"

Startled, Nick slammed down the top to the computer and pulled her down onto his lap. "I must be losing my touch," he told her. "Usually I can sense when someone is coming up behind me."

"Your touch seems pretty good to me," she answered with a soft moan, as Nick worked his magic fingers up her back and into her scalp. "Um, a girl could get used to this."

"And here I thought you liked me for my sense of humor and my great conversational skills? Isn't that what women say they're looking for in a man?"

Charlotte knew he was teasing her, but she did like his sense of humor and great conversational skills. Of course, he had lots of skills she liked, but she decided now wasn't the time to bring them up for fear he would want to act on them.

"I didn't expect you quite so early," Nick told her honestly. "Are you done for the day or do you have another appointment?"

"I'm not only done for the day, but I came to take my two favorite men in the world out to dinner. My treat!"

"You seem pretty happy," Nick said smiling at her. "I take it you had a good day?"

"It was a really good day, and I even brought you a present." Extracting herself from Nick's lap Charlotte reached into her bag and handed him the books from Lydia Wells.

"I'm not really sure what you might have read, but I thought you might enjoy something to do while you're recuperating. Lydia Wells at The Book Nook recommended these, and actually they're a gift from her."

Nick took the package from her hands and unwrapped it. "To be honest, I haven't had much time to read for quite a while, but I used to like it a lot when we were younger." Turning the books over to read the synopsis, Nick smiled and nodded. "It was kind of Lydia to do this, but I don't understand. I mean Geoff is a friend of Pop's, but I hardly know them."

"You're kind of a hero to the Wells," Charlotte told him. "I imagine all of the people who had Tony Neel doing their books feel the same way. I'm just sorry my selfishness kept me from seeing the big picture." Charlotte looked into Nick's eyes and kissed him gently on the lips. "You're my hero too, Special Agent Greyson, and I really, truly hope you will forgive me for all the awful things I said to you the night you came to talk with me."

It wasn't often Nick was at a loss for words, but Charlotte could tell he was struggling right now. "It was never you who I was upset with," he began. "I knew I should have told you before I left after the holiday weekend what was going to eventually happen, but I didn't think we were that close to making an arrest, and I didn't want to lose the magic we were creating. You had every right to be mad at me Charlotte, but I'm thankful that you've given me another chance."

"That night you asked me not to run away from us again, and now I promise you that I won't. We did create magic, Nick, and it's growing inside of me," she said laying his hand on her stomach. "I hope we still have lots of magic left to uncover."

"I love you Lottie," he said gently. "I always have and I always will."

"Gran was right," she told him. "Things do have a way of happening for a reason. Now how about we get Pop and head to the pier! Babycakes and I have a hankering for some shrimp and some mango slaw. And if you have any pull with your child, please ask it to let me keep them down!"

After a relaxing dinner at the City Pier, they arrived back at the marina and Pop stepped out of the car. "Thank you for dinner, Lottie," he told her. "It was an unexpected treat, and I really enjoyed spending time with you and Nick. And thank you too," he continued, "for helping my friends. I'm already hearing good things, and I just appreciate you stepping in to clean up any mess Tony Neel made."

"I'm happy to help in any way I can, Pop, I hope you know that. In fact, I'm enjoying this so much, I've been thinking about opening an actual accounting business, but I want to get all of this straightened out first."

Pop thanked her again and headed inside, leaving Charlotte and Nick alone.

"Will you stay?" he asked with hope in his eyes. Charlotte didn't want to let him down, especially after her big apology earlier, but she had to make him see this was outside of her comfort level.

"Nick," she started. "I know that we're not kids anymore, but it would just feel too weird to me to share a bed with you in your childhood home. It isn't a matter of Pop caring or not caring, but my own sense of values. Please understand."

He nodded but Charlotte could see the dark clouds of hurt starting to form in his eyes, and she didn't ever want to be the reason for those clouds again. "It's just that I really like falling asleep with you in my arms and waking up knowing you're there," he told her. "That isn't something I ever expected to need in my life, but I do, and I'm not ashamed to admit it."

Hot damn, did I hit the mother-lode, or what? she asked herself. Here was this man, so hot that her skin tingled when he touched it, and he loved her and wanted to be with her, and she didn't even have to ask!

"How about we compromise?" she asked him with a devilish gleam in her eyes. "You go pack a few essentials and we'll go back to my house? Actually, I bought you a present today and I was hoping you would use it tonight."

Charlotte could see the wheels turning at the mention of a present to use that night. Obviously, they didn't need condoms, and sex toys

118

seemed out of the question since they hadn't had sex since he'd been released from the hospital. After letting him ponder for a few more minutes, Charlotte opened her purse and gave him his gift.

"A toothbrush?" Nick laughed. "That's about the best present you could have given me. But remember that I said *about*."

"It's to leave at my house, so you're always prepared," she answered. "And in case you didn't know it, having your own toothbrush at a woman's house is one step up from the commitment of that class ring I never got."

Nick held his new toothbrush to his heart and opened the car door. "Let's get my clothes so we can get back to your house. Not only do I want to use my new toothbrush tonight, but I've been dreaming about that fancy shower of yours. Whether you join me or not will be totally up to you."

Chapter 47

Now

When they pulled in the driveway Charlotte looked toward the beach and Mrs. Danvers's house and knew she had to make time to visit with her friend. She hadn't been to see her since before her trip to New Smyrna Beach, and she not only missed her wise older friend, but she felt guilty for not at least calling her while she was in Tampa, waiting for Nick to come out of his coma.

Nick was already out of the car and headed to the door. Charlotte followed suit and unlocked the door to her charming beach bungalow. Without even giving her a chance to put down her things Nick had his arms around her and was placing soft sensual kisses on her neck and shoulders. The heat that was radiating off him was almost overpowering. Charlotte pulled back just long enough to set down her bag and her purse.

Charlotte would have loved a glass of wine, but of course, being pregnant she couldn't drink, and Nick's medication didn't allow for him to consume alcohol either. Needing badly to get her emotions under control she asked him, "Do you want a coke or glass of water?"

She wasn't sure what the noise Nick made was, a growl or a groan, but the answer he gave her made her melt a little more, "The only thing I want is you."

Shit! Shit! Shit! I invited him here, even gave him a toothbrush to leave right alongside mine, so why am I so nervous about the thought of sex?

All these thoughts were swimming around in her brain when Nick pulled her back into his arms and kissed her with all the passion and heat she knew he was so good at. "I'm going to go in and start the shower," he told her with a look of lust in his eyes. "I hope you'll be in to join me."

He pulled his T-shirt over his head, and oh my he was one chiseled hunk of man. Even with the scar from where he'd been shot, still a little pink and angry looking, Nick Greyson's body was a work of art. When he slipped off his shorts and was standing stark naked in her living room, Charlotte gasped as she realized the monster was totally standing at attention, and she was totally terrified.

Before she had a chance to voice her concerns her phone rang, and yes, she was saved by the bell! Nick headed to the shower, and Charlotte held up one finger, as if to say, "Just a minute," and while trying to get her breathing under control, she answered.

Nick was enjoying the big shower head with the massaging jets, but he was clean head to toe and still no Charlotte. He wanted her to come to him on her own without feeling pressured, but the water was starting to cool, even though his desire had not. Finally, he grabbed one of the big fluffy towels she kept on a wicker shelf and grumbling to himself stepped out of the shower and dried off.

To be honest, he was more hurt than anything, so he did his best to rein in his emotions before listening to Charlotte's excuses for why they shouldn't make love. But when he turned off the bathroom light and looked into the bedroom, his heart did a double take. Charlotte lay on the bed, fully clothed, the phone still in her hand, sound asleep.

"I'm such a jerk," Nick muttered to himself. She had told him how tired the pregnancy was making her, and despite that and the awful morning sickness, she had taken on a new job, and was spending her free time with him, when what she needed was some quality time for herself.

He took the phone from her hand, gently removed her shoes, and slipped her pants down her slim legs, all without waking her up. Just the sight of her in a yellow tank top and lacy red panties about did him in, but he took the high road and lifted her legs under the covers.

"Nick?" Charlotte questioned, in a sleep induced state. "What are you doing?"

"I'm putting you to bed," he answered with a gentle kiss to her forehead, and once she was all tucked in, he joined her.

Chapter 48

Now

Sun was streaming through the windows when Charlotte woke up on Wednesday morning. She stretched like a cat lying in a windowsill, and suddenly, the night before flashed in front of her eyes, and she instinctively reached for Nick.

"Looking for me?" came a voice from beside her bed. Charlotte opened her eyes, and there stood Nick in all his masculine glory, wearing nothing but a pair of dark boxer briefs. Nervously she licked her lips as butterflies tickled inside, unfortunately she wasn't sure if it was arousal, or she was about to be sick.

Charlotte scooted to a sitting position so Nick could sit down beside her. "I read online that if you eat crackers before you get out of bed they can keep you from being sick, and peppermint tea is what Maya gives the girls when they have a tummy ache," he said, handing her the crackers and a cup of tea.

"You went online to find out how to help with my morning sickness?" she questioned. "I think that's the nicest thing anyone has ever done for me."

"I'm a nice guy," Nick teased, "and also one who feels badly for not listening better to what you've been telling me. You've had a lot of changes in your life in the last few weeks, and all of them because of me. When we make love again, I want it to be because it's what we both want, and I won't try to talk you into something you're not ready for."

Oh, how she loved this man! Charlotte could feel her cheeks getting pink, so she took a sip of tea and put a cracker in her mouth, in hopes that he wouldn't notice. How did she tell him that she did want to make love with him, she wanted it badly, but her pregnancy hormones and changes in her body had her emotions all out of whack?

"What time is your first appointment this morning?" Nick asked her.

"Ten o'clock," she groaned, "and today's a long day. Since we're going to Tampa tomorrow I have three meetings today, and three again on Friday, and then hopefully, I can start making headway on where everyone stands."

"I'm going to fix myself a cup of your fancy coffee while you shower and dress, and when you get done I'll have some toast and fruit waiting for you, okay? And by the way, who was your evening caller? Anyone I need to be concerned about?"

"Breakfast sounds wonderful and my caller was Hank Phillips, of Phillips' Pet Palace. I told him I'm allergic to cats and asked if we could meet someplace other than his shop. He's going to bring his books and come here. I guess he was just calling to confirm."

Nick envisioned the fifty-year-old bachelor, with a bald head and a pot belly, and decided it was safe for him to come to Charlotte's home. He hated feeling so protective, but besides being head over heels in love with the woman, he had years of FBI training that always made him be cautious.

"If you want me to stay here with you, I'd be happy to," he asked hopefully. "I can just sit on the lanai and read my new book."

"I'm a big girl, Nick," she told him. "I'll be fine. I've known Hank for years, so there's nothing for you to worry about, but I do appreciate that you want to look out for me." In her head, she thought it probably wasn't the right time to tell him about Clay Stevens question about them being an item and her feeling that he was hitting on her.

Nick smiled and nodded. "I'm looking out for both of you," he said, gently caressing her belly. "Now into the shower so you can eat before your client arrives. I called Pop to pick me up, but I want to make sure you're thoroughly clothed before I leave you with another man."

Chapter 49

Now

Charlotte's appointments on Wednesday did not go as well as the ones the day before, and by six thirty that evening, she was dead on her feet. Nick sent her a text saying Pop made spaghetti for dinner and for her to come over whenever she was done for the day. All she truly wanted was a hot bath and her bed. Not wanting to hurt his feelings she drove to the marina with every intention of making a quick getaway. By herself.

Even the best laid plans can go astray when you're hungry, and the aroma of homemade marinara simmering on the stove was enough to change Charlotte's. The table was set for the three of them, and Nick was just putting garlic bread under the broiler when she walked in. It would have been rude to refuse their hospitality, right?

"How was your day, dear?" Nick asked her with a wink.

"Much better now," she teased back. "Domesticity becomes you."

Grabbing her around the waist, Nick gave her a chaste kiss on the lips, but whispered in her ear. "I've always had a fantasy about a woman serving me dinner wearing an apron, and nothing else, but since my dad is here, and it's his kitchen, let's just put it on the back burner for now."

"I've had that same fantasy," Charlotte said, batting her lashes, "only instead of a woman it was a hot, hung, young Adonis."

Nick's eyes got big and laughing he shook his head. "I don't even know how to reply to that." Changing the subject, he asked her, "Are you hungry? Pop is like an Italian grandmother when it comes to making red sauce. There's enough here to feed most of the people on Anna Maria Island."

As tired as she was when she got there, Charlotte felt herself begin to relax and enjoy the easy-going banter with Nick. She had sensed the same lighthearted mood when she visited with Becca and Jared at their home, but it was the first time in her life she had felt it for herself, and damn did it feel good!

Pop came in from the deck and gave her a hug and a kiss on her forehead. "I've got wine or sweet tea, Lottie," he told her. "Pick your poison."

"I'll have some of your yummy sweet tea," she answered him. "Nick, the same for you?"

Pop grabbed the pitcher of tea and a huge bowl of salad out of the refrigerator, just as Nick was pulling the bread out of the oven. "You guys sit down," Charlotte told them, "and I'll serve you."

She could tell that Nick was about to argue, so she gave him a look that told him she meant business. He and Pop took their seats while Charlotte ladled up big helpings of pasta with red sauce for the men, and a small plate of plain noodles with one spoon of sauce for herself. To be honest, she was starving and really wanted more, but not knowing how the spicy sauce would stay down, she decided to error on the side of caution.

"Is that all you're having, Lottie," Pop quizzed her. "That's not enough food to keep a bird alive."

"I had a really big lunch," she fibbed, "and I wasn't going to have dinner at all but it smelled so good I couldn't resist. Now how about passing me the salad?"

Nick could tell by the look on her face that she wasn't being honest, but he also knew why. Hoping to get Charlotte out of the hot seat he started to talk about their plans for the next day.

"So, my doctor's appointments start at ten in the morning, and I need to go by my condo first. I hate that I can't drive us, but if you want to drive the Jeep, Charlotte, we can take it instead of your car."

"Honestly, I think I'm more comfortable driving my car, so what time do you want to leave?"

"Is eight too early?" Nick asked her. "After I see the doctors I need to go see Director James, so I'll need time to change clothes when we get there, and pack some more things to bring back here. I've had enough of athletic wear to last me a lifetime."

"Do you have any idea when you'll be released to go back to work, Nick?" Charlotte asked cautiously. In her mind, she knew, at some point, he would be going back to his job with the FBI, but in her heart, she wanted him to stay in AMI and with her.

Nick shook his head and refused to look her in the eye. "I have no clue," he told her. "It's part of what I need to talk with the doctors about tomorrow."

Shit! Shit! Shit! He wants to get back to work, Charlotte was screaming inside! He almost died, and would never have known about our baby, and he can't wait to leave us and go back to Tampa.

"Speaking of tomorrow," Pop jumped in, seeing the hurt on Charlotte's face, "I'm not going to be able to meet you at Stavros for lunch. I haven't been able to find anyone to hold down the fort for me here, and Noah isn't going to be back anyway, so the two of you can visit with Maya and the girls. We'll do a family thing another day."

At this point, Charlotte was back to being bone weary, only now her heart was hurting as much as her body. Pushing back the plate still covered with food, she stood up and said she needed to go.

"Give me a few minutes and I'll be ready to leave," Nick told her, starring down at the plate of spaghetti he really wanted to finish.

"You eat," Charlotte told him with a forced smile. "I need to do some work at home, so it's probably better if you stay here tonight. I'll be here at eight in the morning to pick you up."

Nick stood up and called after her. "Charlotte…," but she was already out the door.

"Women," he muttered under his breath. "What the fuck just happened?"

Pop came up behind his son and put his hand on his shoulder. "When your mom was pregnant it didn't take much to set her off. I finally learned not to take it personally."

"You know?" Nick asked his father.

"Son, I'm the father of three, and I'm a pretty observant man. I had my suspicions while you were still in a coma, but I knew that when the time was right, I'd be told. So how do you feel about becoming a dad?"

"Like I've been given a gift," Nick said softly. "Charlotte is everything I've ever wanted, and I love her so much, but she's one complicated woman."

Pop laughed and slapped Nick on the back. "They're all complicated, Nick, that's what makes them so fascinating. But from what I know about Charlotte Luce, she's more than worth the energy you're going to have to put in to make a relationship with her work. You'll just have to be patient and persistent, that's all any man can do."

Nick nodded and headed to the kitchen with his plate. "I guess instead of spaghetti tonight, I'm going to be eating crow."

Pop smiled and together they cleaned up the kitchen, with neither one of them wearing an apron.

Chapter 50

Now

Charlotte woke up on Thursday morning with a headache from lack of food the day before and a heartache because Nick wasn't in bed beside her. Reaching over to touch the pillow his head had slept on the previous night, she wondered if they'd ever be able to have a real relationship. He had promised her a talk on the way home from Tampa, so right now, all she could do was get ready and hope the day went well.

Unfortunately, the minute her feet hit the floor, she felt the familiar waves of nausea rumbling through her stomach, and she ran to the bathroom. After a few minutes of the dry heaves, caused from no real nutritional intake after her breakfast yesterday morning, she scraped herself off the floor and into the shower. The hot water did a lot for her dragging spirits, but oh how some saltines and peppermint tea would taste about now.

After combing out her mass of tangled wet curls, Charlotte once again checked her reflection in the mirror, and there it was! The tiniest bit of belly bump stared back at her, and she knew it wasn't from overeating! Oh, how she wanted to call Becca, but the decision on when to tell people was happening today, so she would have to be content to wait a few more hours.

"Hang in there, Babycakes," she said, running a hand over her slightly swollen belly. "Your mom may be a rookie, but your Aunt Becca definitely is not."

Dressed in an Ann Taylor coral oasis dress she had purchased prior to her split with the bank and taupe ballet flats, she felt polished, yet comfortable, and that's what she needed for a day of uncertainties.

Like, was Nick healing the way he needed to be, or were there problems she couldn't see? And if he was okay, when would he be released to go back to work, and when that happened, where did that leave her? She had plans to visit with Shelly while Nick saw his doctors, and she was in real need of advice from her new friend. Not only could she talk openly with Shelly about the baby, but she had a way of seeing what Charlotte couldn't, and oh did she need that right now.

Pulling into the marina parking lot, Charlotte touched her locket instead of heading inside. "Hey Gran, it's me," she said with a sigh. "I really miss you and I just wanted you to know I saw a little baby bump in the mirror this morning, and it both excites me and terrifies me. I want to be the kind of mother you were, but I'm not sure I know how. Anyway, I love you and more than anything I wish you could be here when my baby is born. No, when our baby is born. More than anything I wish you could be here when our baby is born. Nick's and mine."

Charlotte looked up and Nick was standing beside her car door. His hair was still damp from the shower, and his eyes were full of questions she didn't have the answers to. Rolling down the window she asked him, "Are you ready to go?"

Nick walked around the car and got into the passenger seat without taking his focus off her. She knew it would be a long ride to Tampa if she didn't lighten the mood, so she told him of her bout of morning sickness and how she had missed his TLC when she got up. And oh yes! She finally had a baby bump!

"Speaking of baby bumps," he started cautiously, "Pop knows that you're pregnant." Nick looked into her face for a reaction, but Charlotte just smiled.

"I had a feeling he was figuring it out, he always was able to uncover a secret. He won't tell though, will he?" she asked. "He knows that we want to tell people in our own time?"

Nick laughed. "Not only can my dad uncover a secret, but he can keep one, as well, and he knows not to say anything. Although on a different subject he did tell me to say, "Hello," to that sweet Shelly at the hospital. What's that all about?"

Charlotte had no idea, but it was definitely something she intended to find out!

Chapter 51

Now

The drive to Tampa was uneventful, with the conversation staying neutral and not veering to personal issues. Nick didn't bring up Charlotte's mini meltdown from the night before and neither did she. When they arrived at his condominium complex, they walked in hand in hand, as if they didn't have a care in the world, but the minute Nick unlocked the door, he froze.

Looking around his living room he scrubbed his hands over his face before saying a word. "This has been my home for six years," he told her, "and it never occurred to me that I might not be safe here. What I realize now, is that in my job, there really is no safe place."

Charlotte put her arms around him and let him rest his head against hers. She had no words of comfort, but at least she was there for him to lean on.

As they walked down the hall to Nick's bedroom, he asked her about when he was in the hospital, and when she had stayed there with his dad and brother. "So, Pop told me that you got to sleep in my bed, it's pretty great, isn't it? This is the only bed I've ever had where my feet don't hang over the end, and I have lots of room to move around."

Charlotte looked at the California king, and mentally agreed that it was just the right size for someone with Nick's six-foot five-inch height, but when she envisioned him having room to move around, she remembered the dream she had when she slept there, and all of a sudden, the bed looked more like a torture chamber.

"Nick?" Charlotte asked quietly, "how many women have slept in this bed with you? Let me rephrase that, how many women have you brought to this bed?"

Nick looked shell-shocked. "What?" he demanded.

"It's a pretty straight-forward question," she answered, crossing her arms, "the night I slept here I couldn't quit thinking about all the woman who had enjoyed this big bed with you, and I even ended up having a terrible dream about it. You know about my past, now I need to know about yours."

Nick looked out the window, trying to come up with an answer that would appease her and not have her walking out the door. After the episode at dinner last night, he knew how easily she could come unglued, and it was the last thing that he wanted.

"Charlotte, you are the love of my life, and I would do anything to make you happy, but I don't think you'll like anything that I tell you. Maybe this isn't a good conversation for us to have, especially when I'll be having my blood pressure taken in about thirty minutes."

Right before his eyes, strong determined Charlotte wilted, and it broke Nick's heart. He reached out to pull her in for a hug, but she was having none of it.

"I'm going to wait in the other room while you change and pack," she told him, trying to keep her voice from breaking. "We aren't going to make it across town if we don't hurry."

Twice in less than twenty-four hours she had walked away from him, and Nick had no idea how to make it better. "Patience and persistence, right, Dad?" he spoke to no one, and then because she was right about the time, he changed and threw a few things in a suitcase.

Nick came out of the bedroom expecting to find Charlotte waiting in the living room, but when he walked by the guestroom—the one his nieces called the butterfly room, he found her sitting on one of the pink covered twin beds—holding a baby doll in her arms.

"You'll be a great dad," she told him with eyes still damp with tears.

"I had the best to learn from," he replied, sitting down beside her.

Charlotte nodded and ran her hand down his chest, unaccustomed to seeing him in a suit and tie. "You clean up good, Special Agent," she told him, as she allowed him to take her in his arms.

"We have plans to talk on the way home, right?" he asked her. "If you still want to know about my life before you came back into it, I'll tell you, but the one thing you need to know right now is you are the only woman I've ever said I love you to, and you're the only one who's ever been able to turn my world upside down."

Charlotte smiled, happy at least for now with his answer. She kissed his cheek and led him towards the door. "I can't ever sleep in that bed with you," she smirked, "so if you have any plans about me staying here, you're going to need to get a new one."

Nick shook his head and followed her out the door. If a new bed could fix this, he was in.

Chapter 52

Now

"Oh, Charlotte you look wonderful!" Shelly Bert squealed as she hugged her friend. "I feel like I haven't seen you in forever, and it's been less than two weeks. I can't wait to hear all about the reunion with Special Agent Greyson; get in here and start dishing."

Charlotte followed Shelly into her office and wondered, where do I begin? "Well," she started slowly, "to be honest, it's been a little bit of a rollercoaster ride. I came here today all prepared to ask you if Nick's meds could be causing him anxiety, because he was running hot and cold with his temperament, but the last few days he's been acting more like himself. I, on the other hand, am a complete mess and seem to fly off the handle at every little thing."

Charlotte put her head in her hands and continued. "I didn't want to bother you when I know you're so busy, but not being able to tell anyone about the baby is really taking its toll on me. I'm still having intermittent morning sickness; I'm so tired some days I can hardly stay awake to get ready for bed, and I could cry at the drop of a hat. Tell me, am I going crazy, or is this normal?"

Shelly smiled and looked Charlotte in the eye. "You're having normal first trimester occurrences, Charlotte, but they shouldn't last much longer. Did you talk with Dr. Stanley about how you're feeling? He's really a very compassionate and caring man."

"And a damn fine looking one, too!" Charlotte exclaimed. "You might have given me a heads-up about him being so young and gorgeous, because Nick coerced me into letting him go with me to the appointment, and it could have gone better. We did talk a little about my morning sickness, but with trying to keep Nick in line, I forgot about everything else"

Shelly giggled like a schoolgirl. "So, your big handsome boyfriend wasn't too keen on watching another man looking up your skirt, so to speak? Well, I doubt if it's the first time Dr. Stanley has been faced with a situation like that, and I'm sure it won't be his last. The important thing is the baby is doing well, and you're getting the support from Nick you need."

Charlotte went on to tell her about Nick bringing her crackers and tea, and how he really was taking care of her. Stopping a few minutes before going on, she blurted out. "I'm scared to make love with him, Shelly, and I'm afraid it's a big part of the tension between us. I know that he wants to, and I do too, and even though Dr. Stanley said it was okay, I panic every time I think we're headed that way. What's wrong with me?"

Shelly knelt in front of Charlotte and took hold of her hands. "Charlotte, you and Nick have been through so much in the last two months, it's natural that you're apprehensive about being intimate with him, but I feel as if there's something you aren't saying."

Charlotte could feel the color rising on her face, but she knew that other than Becca, Shelly was the only person she could discuss this with. Clearing her throat and willing herself to speak she said, "Nick is really well endowed. I mean really well, and I keep thinking that sex might hurt the baby or hurt me."

Shelly turned a little pale before she spoke. "Please don't feel this is disrespectful to you or to Nick. Remember that he was a patient here, and I kind of saw…" Shelly struggled to complete her sentence.

"You saw Nick naked?" Charlotte questioned. "Well of course you did, you and all those young nurses you employ around here. I hadn't even given it a thought, but at least you know up-close and personal what I'm talking about."

"Please don't be upset, Charlotte," Shelly continued. "I would never have mentioned it if you hadn't brought the subject up. What's important is for you to remember that your body was designed to hold and protect that little bundle, and while sex might not be advised in

136

some high-risk pregnancies, at this point in yours, there shouldn't be any reason why you and Nick can't enjoy a healthy sex life. Dr. Stanly would have told you if he had concerns. I guess the only other thing I can say is, Congratulations?"

It took Charlotte a minute to realize what Shelly was implying, and once she did she blushed all over again. "I secretly call it The Anaconda, but let's keep that between us."

Once all the pregnancy topics were taken care of, Charlotte asked Shelly if anything was new with her and remembered the message from Pop. "I almost forgot," Charlotte teased her friend, "Pop says to tell that sweet Shelly, Hello. What went on between the two of you that I missed?"

Now it was Shelly's turn to blush. "Nothing went on between us," she protested. "I just overheard him having a conversation with Nick's mom and realized he was hurting. We may have talked a little, but that's all."

Charlotte grinned. "You know Nick's dad is like the father I never had, and I would love to see him have someone in his life. He's spent way too many years alone, or mooning over his ex-wife, and I think you could be just what the doctor ordered."

"Oh, for heaven's sake, Charlotte," Shelly replied. "He's a lovely man who needed a kind touch, but I'm sure that's all I was to him. You have enough going on with your own love life, don't worry about one for me. And speaking of your love life, and not that it's any of my business, but have you and Nick talked about marriage?"

"Don't try to change the subject, my friend, you like him, I can tell. And as for my relationship with Nick, we haven't put any labels on it yet."

Just then Nick returned from seeing Dr. Copeland, his heart surgeon. "I'm going down to have a CT scan," he told the women, "and after Dr. Rivers evaluates it, he'll talk with me and I'll be ready to go."

Noticing both women were doing their best not to laugh, Nick looked confused and asked, "What's so funny?" Neither Charlotte nor Shelly answered.

"Do you want me to go down with you for the CT scan?" Charlotte asked. "I'm sure that Shelly needs to get back to work anyway."

Still not sure what the cause of amusement was, Nick nodded to Charlotte. "I would like you to be there with me unless you have something else you want to do. Dr. Copeland says that I'm doing remarkably well, but it's the head trauma she's still concerned about."

Charlotte could see the worry in Nick's eyes when he talked about his health, so she hugged her friend good-bye with a promise to call her soon. Before she stepped out of Shelly's office, Charlotte turned around and asked her friend, "Any message back to that lovely man?"

Shelly crossed her arms over her chest as if she was angry, but she whispered to Charlotte, "Tell him I said Hello, back."

Chapter 53

Now

Nick and Charlotte were both in good spirits when they arrived at the FBI building after his doctor's appointments. Nick received a good evaluation from both doctors, and thankfully, his head injury was healing nicely. Charlotte felt as if the weight of the world had been lifted after her conversation with Shelly.

"I won't be very long," Nick told her as he stepped out of the car. "I just need to give Director James an update on my progress and see if he'll relinquish Tony Neel's computer."

"That's fine," Charlotte said, "take as much time as you need. I'll wait here and call Becca or send some texts."

"No way," Nick answered her, as he opened the drivers-side door. "Every man going in and out of this building would stop to see if the beautiful lady needed help, and that's just not happening. Besides," he said pulling her to her feet, "I told Director James you'd be coming with me."

"Uh, Nick," Charlotte said with a distressed look on her face. "I need to tell you something about a conversation I had with your boss the day you were taken to the hospital."

Nick laughed out loud before answering. "Oh, I know all about it," he told her with a kiss to her hand. "I think that's part of why he wants to see you now. He was pretty impressed with your spunk, but make sure you tell him no if he offers you a job!"

Shit! Shit! Shit! Charlotte thought. When am I going to learn to keep my big mouth shut!

Just as Nick predicted, the visit with Director James was short and sweet, and he was very cordial to Charlotte. No job offer was made but he did tell Charlotte that it had taken a lot of courage for her to stand up to him, and he admired her conviction. He even gave Nick possession of Tony Neel's computer, saying it had been thoroughly scrubbed and only contained information pertaining to his accounting clients on the island.

"Do you have any idea when you'll be released to come back to work, Nick?" Director James asked as they were leaving his office.

Charlotte held her breath and was very relieved when Nick handed the director signed medical leave paperwork from Dr. Rivers, stating that he couldn't return to the FBI until at least after his next appointment, and that was four weeks away. Director James nodded, shook Nick's hand, and told him to stay in touch.

They were just about to leave when Charlotte heard some serious cat calls. Turning around Nick saw several of his FBI team members standing there, whistling at Charlotte. He did his best to stare them down but couldn't keep a straight face for long.

"We thought you were a figment of old Grey's imagination, but damn if he wasn't telling the truth. You are one seriously sizzling babe!" shouted one of the agents.

A seriously sizzling babe? Her? Maybe she needed to go back and talk to Deputy Director James about a job offer after all?

Nick gave her a very seductive kiss and yelled out to his friends. "And she's all mine."

Chapter 54

Now

They held hands all the way to Maya's house, only letting go to get out of the car. Nick even held on as he knocked on the door but had to let go when they were met with two identical beauties, both vying for attention.

"Uncle Nick, Miss Lottie!" screamed Nikki and Steffi, Maya's twin daughters. "Come see what we have in the back yard. It's a puppy!" they squealed together, leaving Nick and Charlotte laughing along behind them.

"His name is Socrates, after the Greek philosopher," Nikki said as she tried to catch her breath.

"But we're calling him Socs," chimed in Steffi, "because he's an American dog."

Charlotte looked at the wiggling bundle of golden fur, and he immediately had her heart. She had always wanted a pet growing up, but her mom had said dogs were too much work, and her allergies had kept her from having a cat.

Despite her designer dress, Charlotte plopped down on the grass beside the crate and asked the girls, "May I hold him?"

The girls nodded in unison and Charlotte reached in for the chubby squirming puppy.

"Hello, Socs," she told him as she nestled him to her neck. "You sure are a handsome guy."

Charlotte looked up at Nick and saw the total look of love in his eyes. He could tell Charlotte and his nieces were going to be fast friends, and now it appeared the dog would be as well. He was just about to ask for a turn with Socs when Maya came out into the yard.

"Ladies, what have I told you about letting strangers in the house?" she teased them, but then immediately gave her brother a great big hug.

"You look so good, Nick," she told him. Turning to hug Charlotte she said, "You're absolutely glowing, Lottie. Is there a secret routine I should know about?"

Both Charlotte and Nick did their best to look away but Charlotte replied. "Just having Nick better and being able to sleep at night has been a big help. The last time you saw me we were all under a lot of stress." And I'm overflowing with pregnancy hormones, she wanted to say, but that was a conversation for another time.

Maya seemed to buy her story, and linking her arms between them, she told the girls it was time to put Socs away and head over to Stavros for lunch.

Charlotte loved the quaint Greek restaurant Maya and her husband, Dimitri, owned in Tarpon Springs. The first time Nick had taken her there, she had eaten her way through mounds of Greek delicacies, but today she was worried what the flavors and spices might do to her often-nauseated stomach.

Dimi met them at the restaurant, and again, it was hugs all around. "I hope you won't be disappointed with the menu, but Maya wanted me to be able to sit and relax while we ate, so we're having more of an American type lunch instead of one of my Greek specialties."

Inwardly Charlotte gave a sigh of relief and was thrilled when a server brought a platter of cold roasted chicken, cheese, beautiful black grapes, and of course, Kalamata olives. There were also fresh pitas, some grainy looking bread, plus condiments and veggies for sandwiches. What excited Charlotte the most was the bowl of potato chips that was placed right in front of her. She loved chips, but rarely allowed herself to indulge, but today the salty, crispy treat was calling her name.

"So," Maya started, piling a slice of bread with meat and cheese, "since we couldn't have a family lunch today, I was thinking we could have a friends and family dinner here, next weekend to celebrate your recovery, Nick. Noah will be back from his fishing tournament and it should give everyone enough time to make their plans. What do you say?"

Nick took a big gulp of the lemonade in front of him and answered his sister. "I think it sounds great," he told her, "but like a lot of work for you. Are you sure it won't be too much trouble?"

"We want to do this, Nick," she told him honestly. "There are so many people who love you and were rooting for you, and I just want to get them all in the same place at the same time."

Nick looked over at Charlotte, and when she nodded, he answered his sister. "Then I would be honored," he told her, and leaned in and kissed her cheek. "You're the best Mama Bear, and I really mean it."

The rest of the visit was spent planning Nick's celebration dinner, playing with Socs, and introducing Charlotte to Nikki's and Steffi's dollies. By the time they were ready to leave, Charlotte's heart was overflowing with love for Nick's family, and anticipation for the conversation she and Nick had planned for the ride home. The blessing of the day was she hadn't been sick at all, and her stomach wasn't even jumpy. Well not from morning sickness anyway.

Chapter 55

Now

Charlotte was mentally verbalizing what she wanted to discuss with Nick when he told her to turn right and pull into the first parking lot on your left. "Mooberry Frozen Yogurt?" she questioned. "Didn't we just have a big lunch?"

Nick winked and helped her out of the car. "I had a big lunch," he told her. "You had some chicken and some potato chips. Mooberry's isn't Two Scoops, but its darn close, and I think Babycakes needs to try it."

Charlotte shrugged and followed him in. "We'll have an extra-large cup of vanilla with fresh strawberries and granola, and two spoons, please." Nick told the young woman taking their order. Charlotte was about to question why such a big sundae when she noticed the girl looking Nick up and down like he was the newest item on the menu, so she linked her arm with his instead and smiled.

The situation back in control, Nick paid for the froyo and led Charlotte back to the car. "I thought we could take our dessert to the park by the Sunshine Skyway bridge. We can talk privately and safely."

Charlotte agreed knowing their conversations did have a way of becoming heated, and the last thing she wanted to do was wreck her car. She kept it in pristine condition ever since her mom had given it to her during her senior year at IU, and she intended to keep it that way.

Nick directed her to the park and within minutes they were seated at a picnic table in the shade, looking out at the beautiful blue waters of Tampa Bay.

"This is lovely, Nick," Charlotte told him. He lifted a bite of the fruity frozen concoction to her lips, and with strawberry juice dribbling down her chin she said, "and the yogurt is lovely as well."

"Okay, woman, what do we talk about first?" Nick asked her.

Charlotte giggled at the way he said woman so she put her finger on her bottom lip, and tried to be sultry as she answered, "Well, let's see."

They had pretty much already covered the situation with Tony and Carol Neel's arrest, and although Charlotte was still hurt that it had happened the way that it had, she was at peace with the situation and knew Nick had only done what was right for everyone else involved.

"So, next on the agenda is telling our family and friends about the baby," Nick said. "Now that Pop knows, and we know everything is fine with you, and my progress is ahead of schedule, I don't see any reason to put it off, do you?"

Charlotte agreed that it was time to share the news, and the first person on her list to talk to was Becca. She was so lost in thought about the conversation with her best friend she almost missed what Nick said next.

"I promised to tell you about my life these last few years, and I will if you want me to, but to be honest I don't think it's a great idea. It's up to you though." Nick looked into Charlotte's glass green eyes and wished he knew what was going on behind them. The afternoon had been so good that he didn't want anything to spoil it, but a promise was a promise.

"I'm good," Charlotte told him, "and as long as I don't ever get invited into your big bed of babes, I don't need to know a thing."

Nick groaned. "You either don't have much faith in my moral code or your imagination is bigger than my bed. I haven't been a saint these past twelve years, Charlotte, but I haven't exactly been a sinner, either."

"Then let's put this conversation to rest. I can't help but be a little envious of any woman you've known that wasn't me, but I trust you when you say I'm the only one you've ever loved. We both have a past, but that's part of what made us who we are today, so let's just focus on the future. Deal?"

145

Bestowing her with one of his earth-shattering kisses, he answered, "Deal."

At that moment, Charlotte's cell phone rang, and looking down at the caller ID, she laughed.

"You always did have great timing, Becca," she said, and accepted the call from the one person she needed more than anything to talk to.

Chapter 56

Now

Nick listened to the one-sided conversation between Charlotte and Becca, smiling at how wonderful it was to hear the joy in Charlotte's voice as she talked with her friend, but the one thing he didn't hear was anything about her pregnancy. Right before hanging up he heard Charlotte say, "I can't wait," and then she looked at him as if he was a dark chocolate Dove bar!

"Becca and the kids are coming to the Island this weekend and staying all next week!" she shrieked. "We can tell her in person about Babycakes. I'm just so excited, won't it be fun?"

Nick wasn't sure fun was the right word for telling an almost Catholic Nun that he had gotten her best friend pregnant, but he was up for the challenge, whatever it might be. "It will be great to see Becca, but isn't her husband coming? I'd really like to meet the man who talked Sister Rebecca Rose out of a habit and into a home."

"Jared is away doing his last Doctors Without Borders assignment before the baby comes, but he'll be here on Thursday, and I want you to meet him, too. He's such a loving and caring person, and I really think you'll hit it off. You know they came to the hospital when you were first shot and stayed for a couple of days. Jared knew your doctors and the hospital routine, and it was such a blessing to all of us."

Nick nodded, more curious than ever to meet the famous Dr. Tyler but decided to focus on Becca's upcoming visit. "So, what are your plans?" he asked. "If you and Becca want some girl time I'm sure Pop would help me keep an eye on her kids."

"You really are a very nice guy, Nicholas Greyson, but let me talk with Becca and get back with you, okay? I would imagine Grandma

Huddleston will call dibs on the kids, but your offer is pretty amazing."
Charlotte gave his hand a big squeeze and finished the rest of the frozen
yogurt sundae by herself.

"I thought we were going to share that," Nick joked, but secretly,
he was thrilled to see her eating without turning green afterwards.
"Oops, you missed a bite," he told her, licking a bite of melting yogurt
from her fingers, and then hand in hand, they walked back to
Charlotte's car, both pleased with the way their afternoon had turned
out.

The drive home over the Sunshine Skyway Bridge was beautiful
and quiet, as they were both lost in their own thoughts. Charlotte was
thinking about her upcoming visit with Becca, and the announcement
of her pregnancy, and Nick was thinking of how he could keep that
smile on the face of the woman he loved.

Chapter 57

Now

Thursday was a long day for both of them, and after a dinner of carry-out baked potato soup, Charlotte and Nick climbed into her bed with no expectations of anything other than a good night's sleep. Charlotte had appointments with Parker and Erin Miller, of Miller's Bike Rentals, and Kim Le, of Le's Oriental Grocery, on Friday and hoped to meet with Pop late that afternoon. With numbers dancing in her head, she was asleep the moment it hit the pillow.

The day was a little bit of a mixed bag; the Millers had put full trust in Tony Neel and were clueless about their finances, but Kim Le was a very astute young man, and had only used Tony as a resource. He had good records for Charlotte to look over. By the time she arrived at the marina, and her appointment with Pop, she was feeling pretty good about the job she had signed on for, and she realized, overall, she was feeling pretty good as well. Was it possible her morning sickness was a thing of the past?

"Anybody home?" she hollered into the empty marina. Receiving no reply, she stepped out onto the dock, and there were Pop and Nick swimming in the waters of the crystal blue Gulf of Mexico. Nick had been a star swimmer in high school and in college, but it had been years since she had seen him in competition mode. Watching his strong body glide through the water made her stomach do summersaults, and she smiled with anticipation of his climb out of the water. Nick Greyson in swim trunks was always a sight to behold.

"Lottie, you're here," Pop said. "Nick was feeling the need for some exercise, and I didn't want him to be out here alone. Grab a glass of tea or some lemonade and get comfortable while I change."

As Pop climbed out of the water, Charlotte recognized he was still a very fit and attractive man. She didn't want to forget that she had a message back to him from Shelly, and she couldn't wait to see his face when she relayed it. Maybe it wasn't too late for both of these special people to find love again.

Nick swam back to the dock and climbed out of the water. His hair had grown longer in the past few weeks, and when he gave his head a shake, you would have thought he was preening for the camera. Charlotte handed him his towel but stayed right in front of the step so he had to touch her to get by.

"This is the kind of treatment a man could get used to," Nick teased her. "I've really gotten out of shape so I decided swimming might be a good workout to start with. Maya's suit's still in her room, care to join me?" The look he gave her was dangerous and she decided it was time to walk away.

"Your dad and I have an appointment, so as much fun as that sounds, I'm going to have to pass." She was wearing red crop pants and a white T-shirt, but it didn't stop Nick from smacking her backside with his towel. "Hey!" Charlotte cried. "I'm going to tell your dad that you're not playing nice," and with a big grin on her face she went inside.

Chapter 58

Now

"So, tell me," Charlotte began as she sat at the kitchen table with Pop, "just what all did Tony do for you, and what are your expectations from me?" It was pretty much the same question she had started out asking all the small business owners that Tony Neel had worked for, and it gave her a good segue into the conversation about their personal records, or lack of them. Because of the situation Pop had gotten into with his loan payments, Charlotte was not prepared for his answer.

Pop was looking down at the table, and seemed a little embarrassed, but he answered Charlotte honestly. "Until last year all Tony did for me was my quarterly tax returns. I've taken care of the finances on this place since I was twenty-five, so paying someone to do them for me just didn't make sense."

Charlotte was confused. She knew Pop had helped Nick get closer to Tony and his illegal activities, but she couldn't believe that he had purposely defaulted on his loan. She was about to ask him for clarification when he spoke up.

"Sometime last year Nick called me and asked if I could get closer to Tony Neel. He wouldn't elaborate but said that he was investigating an intercontinental gambling ring, and Tony's name had come up." Charlotte could tell Pop was uncomfortable, but she needed to know more.

"Anyway," he continued, "we decided I would quit making my loan payments for several months so it gave Nick a plausible reason to come home and check out what was going on. We weren't trying to hurt you Lottie, and I never would have let the bank foreclose on this marina. Next to my family, this place means everything to me."

Charlotte put her head in her hands and nodded. When she looked up, Nick was standing by his dad, ready to step in if he was needed. She could see the worried look in his eyes, knowing this was the issue that had come between them right after the July 4th holiday.

"I understand, Pop, I do," she told her surrogate father. "Tony Neel is behind us now, and you did what you needed to do to help Nick stop some bad people. What I need to know is what you really need from me?"

Pop smiled and Nick let out the breath he was holding, and together they decided what kind of accounting expertise Charlotte could supply. She wanted the whole Tony Neel episode to go away for good, but in her heart, she didn't think it ever could. Would Nick have to testify when his trial came up? Were there more arrests to be made, and if so, would Nick be a part of them? Right now would be a perfect time for a cold bottle of Beach House wine, but that couldn't happen. *Shit! Shit! Shit!* she thought, how did a geeky numbers girl like me get caught up in so much drama?

Chapter 59

Now

Pop got up from the table and opened the refrigerator. "Who's up for leftover spaghetti?" he asked. "I don't think any of us enjoyed it on Wednesday."

Charlotte blushed and Nick grinned as they got up and helped Pop recreate the uneaten Italian feast. This time she planned to enjoy the meal without any hormonal outbursts!

After they ate and cleaned up the kitchen, Charlotte took Nick aside and asked if he was ready to go. "Becca's coming in the morning, and I need to do some laundry and get a good night's rest," she told him.

Nick pulled her in for a hug before replying. "I'm going to stay here tonight," he said, gently kissing the top of her head.

Charlotte didn't know how to answer, so she pulled away and looked up at his face. "Is everything okay, Nick? Are you upset about something?"

"Everything is fine," he assured her, "but Noah's coming in late tonight, and I want to tell him about the baby before Pop or I slip and say something. Then first thing tomorrow morning, I'm going to call Maya, and the Greyson clan will have all been duly notified. How about you, any thoughts about when you're going to tell your mom?"

Charlotte blew out the breath she'd been holding in and shook her head. "It's not like she can say much, but I'm pretty certain this is not what she expected from me. But telling Becca is my first priority, and that's going to happen during our time together tomorrow."

"Speaking of tomorrow," Nick said with a sly smile. "I hope you haven't made a lot of plans for the day, because I have something for the two of you to do." He pulled two pieces of paper out of his back pocket and handed them to Charlotte.

"Spa appointments, Nick?" she shouted. "You arranged for Becca and me to have a full day spa treatment at the Sea-renity Spa? Oh, my gosh, I can't believe it! I haven't had a massage in ages, but do you have any idea how much a full day session costs?"

Nick laughed. "As a matter of fact, I do, so don't be getting used to it. I wanted you and Becca to have a special day together., I take it you approve?"

Charlotte threw her arms around him and gave him a huge kiss of appreciation. "This is a wonderful surprise Nick, and I know how much Becca will enjoy it. I have a feeling she doesn't have time for a lot of pampering while taking care of her brood, but they're safely with Grandma tomorrow, so this will be perfect!"

Holding hands, Nick walked Charlotte to her car and made sure she was buckled in. "I'll miss you tonight," she told him, "but I'm glad you're going to have some time with Noah."

"Will you and Becca stop by on your way to Bridge Street tomorrow? I'd really like to say hello and thank her for coming to the hospital," Nick replied.

"My plan is to get up and take a run on the beach and then pick Becca up at her mom's around eight. We'll have just enough time for a quick stop if we're going to make our appointments by nine. Oh, I'm so excited about tomorrow, and I can't wait to go home and call Becca."

"Let me know when you get safely locked in your house tonight and be careful running in the morning. You haven't done it in a while; be sure to stretch before you take off and start out slowly."

"Yes Dad," Charlotte said with a grin. Putting her car in reverse, she added, "I really love you, Nick Greyson, I really, really do."

Chapter 60
Now

It felt good to be up early and on the beach. There were no repercussions from the spaghetti feast the night before, but Charlotte was determined not to take any chances; even though her Keurig was calling her name. Deciding that staying away from coffee was the right thing to do, she grabbed a bottle of water instead and vowed to forgo coffee from her favorite morning ritual, at least for a little while more.

Following Nick's advice, she stretched out and warmed her muscles before starting a slow jog by the water. Even though it was just after six o'clock, the beach was full of activity, and she loved watching the other people running or walking or just enjoying the early morning sun.

One couple in particular caught her eye, and she was mesmerized by how in love they seemed. Holding hands as they leisurely strolled, Charlotte guessed they were in their eighties, at least. She wondered to herself where she and Nick would be in fifty years, and silently prayed it was right here, on their beloved beach, on Anna Maria Island.

After a good run, Charlotte was feeling the heat and decided to walk for a while to cool down. As she passed Mrs. Danvers cottage, she saw her friend out watering the flowers on her porch and knew she needed to stop. She'd find some way to make up the time, but it had been ages since she'd seen her and this was a perfect opportunity to say hello.

"Charlotte, my dear," Mrs. D. began, "it's so good to see you. I was beginning to think I'd never see you on this beach again. I heard about the nonsense with the bank, and of course, everyone's been talking about the Neels and Nicholas Greyson's son. I was hoping it didn't mean I would lose my friend and favorite neighbor."

Charlotte smiled and gave Mrs. D. a soft kiss on the cheek. "I have so much to tell you, and I wish I could stay and visit, but my oldest friend Becca Tyler is in town, and I promised to pick her up at eight. You remember Becca, don't you? She was Becca Huddleston before she got married."

"I do remember your friend, Charlotte. The two of you used to swim right outside my cottage when you were girls. Leo and I loved watching you frolic in the water and build sea turtles in the sand. It seems like yesterday even though it's been years."

It seemed like yesterday to Charlotte too, and she made a mental note to bring Becca and her kids by to see Mrs. Danvers while they were in town. "I hate to leave," Charlotte admitted to her elderly friend, "but I promise I'll be back this week, okay?"

"And will you be bringing contraband?" Mrs. Danvers asked with a sly smile.

"You bet!" Charlotte answered. "You get the ice tea ready and I'll bring the Chinese. Sesame Chicken or Chicken Lo Mein?"

"Surprise me," Mrs. Danvers giggled, and with a kiss and a hug, Charlotte was off.

Chapter 61

Now

"Dammit!" Charlotte exclaimed as she tried to button her favorite skort. "I know I haven't gained enough weight not to be able to get into my clothes, Babycakes, so what's going on?" Looking at herself in the mirror, Charlotte could see that her baby bump was getting bigger, and all she could think was that the baby growing inside of her was going to be a big one, just like it's dad. Going instead with a pink and white sundress, her belly was covered and hopefully not noticeable! White flip flops and her locket completed the outfit, and soon she was on her way to Becca's parent's home.

It was just eight o'clock when Charlotte arrived at the Huddleston's, and not knowing who might still be sleeping, she knocked softly on the door. As soon as her hand hit the door, Becca opened it, and the two friends hugged like long lost family. Of course, that's the way it always was when they saw each other, their bond being thicker than blood.

"I'm so excited about today!" Becca exclaimed. I haven't had a full day at a spa since right before my wedding, and you know how long that's been. Either Nick is just really extravagant, or he thinks he owes me something. Which is it?" she laughed.

"To be honest, I don't know much about his financial situation, but he has a nice condo in Tampa and drives a new Jeep, so hopefully he's paid well," answered Charlotte. "I guess maybe it's something we need to discuss, but I really think today is just about him wanting to do something nice for us. He knows we don't see each other very often, and he's a good guy, Bec. How did I ever forget that?"

Becca nodded as she put her arm around her friend and led her away from the house. "We didn't get in until about seven thirty last night, and with all the excitement, the kids didn't settle down until after ten, so they're still asleep. Mom and Dad are having coffee on the lanai, so let's make a break for it while we can. I'm anxious to see all three of the Greyson men, so I hope they're early risers!"

Becca had just seen Noah and Pop a few weeks earlier at the hospital, but the smile on Nick's face when she and Charlotte walked in, melted her heart. "I'm really glad that Nick is back in your life Lottie," Becca told her. "Nick was my friend too and I've really missed him."

"Sister Rebecca Rose," Nick said softly, trying to swallow the lump in his throat. "You sure grew up to be one beautiful lady."

Becca grabbed him around the neck and hugged him for dear life. "You ought to see me when I'm not pregnant," she teased. "I'm even better. But for some reason I seem to be pregnant most of the time!"

Charlotte shot Nick a look that said, "I haven't told her yet," and he looked back with a wink that said he understood. "Well at least you're wearing shoes," was his retort to Becca, and with that they all laughed.

"So, where's that brother of yours and your foxy dad? I was hoping to see them this morning, too," Becca questioned.

"Noah has a problem with his boat so he and Pop took it for a spin in the bay. They thought they would be back before you got here, but if you don't see them this morning, I know they want to see you while you're in town." Nick smiled at her again and added, "You really do look great Becca, and I can't tell you how good it feels to stand in this room with two of my favorite women of all time."

"We're two of how many?" Charlotte chimed in, acting as if she was mad.

"Well, let's see," Nick said, putting his finger on his chin like he was thinking. "There's Maya, and the twins of course, and I guess I need to add my mom…."

"Okay, we get it big guy," Charlotte grinned. "And just for the record, you are one of our favorite men of all time, although our list is way longer than yours."

Nick grabbed her around the waist, and Charlotte giggled, while Becca just smiled. "I can't believe that after all this time you two are finally together," she laughed, "I wasn't sure I would ever see this day."

Chapter 62

Now

"Nick looks so good, Lottie," Becca said as they were heading to Bradenton Beach and the Sea-renity Spa. "I don't mind telling you that Jared was really concerned if Nick would ever fully recover, but he looks amazing. There were a lot of prayers at work here, and I'm so thankful they were answered the way we asked for them to be."

"Do you ever think about how your life would have been if you'd actually entered the convent?" Charlotte asked quietly. She knew how much Becca loved her family, but she also knew how much she had wanted to be a nun.

"You've heard it said that the Lord works in mysterious ways, right? I believe with all my heart that his plan all along was for Jared and me to meet and get married, otherwise it couldn't have worked like it did. I still love the church, but now I'm serving it differently." Becca had such a peaceful look on her face that Charlotte had to agree that bringing Jared Tyler and Rebecca Huddleston together, was nothing short of divine intervention.

Knowing the time had come for her to tell Becca about her pregnancy, Charlotte took a big breath and then started in on her carefully rehearsed speech. It wasn't like Becca would think less of her for being an unwed mother, but still Charlotte felt a little uncomfortable sharing her news. "So how is Baby Tyler doing?" Charlotte asked as a segue into her news

"Doing great!" Becca exclaimed, "How is Baby Greyson doing?" she asked, with a straight face.

"What? How…? You know?" she asked her friend, with an absolute look of horror on her face.

Shit, Shit, Shit! How can this be? Charlotte asked herself.

"Oh, Lottie, we've known each other for twenty-five years…. Do you think I haven't figured you out in all that time?" Becca answered with a smile. "For the last month, every time we've talked, you've asked little questions about being pregnant that you never asked with the other three. But what really confirmed my suspicions was seeing you today. Your boobs are about to pop out of that dress, and when we hugged, I felt a little bump in your tummy that you've never had before. And girlfriend, you're absolutely glowing, and pregnancy hormones are the only thing I know of that does that to a woman."

Charlotte wanted to pull the car over and have a real heart to heart with her friend, but she knew if she did that they'd be late for their appointments, and oh how she needed the relaxation of the spa!

"So, what do you think?" Charlotte asked timidly. "Are you disappointed in me?"

"There is nothing you could ever do to disappoint me, Charlotte Luce. You are one of the strongest and most loving people I've ever known, and if you and Nick are happy about this pregnancy, then I am too. You are happy, right?"

Charlotte nodded, trying to keep the tears at bay. "I never honestly thought I'd be a mother, but this baby, and Nick, mean everything to me. I made so many mistakes with him before, Becca, and I'm just so thankful to have an opportunity to make things right."

"I hope you're not taking the blame for what happened at the sendoff, Lottie," Becca scolded. "I know you told me what happened, and why Ashley was in the pool house with Nick, but there was a lot going on in that room, and you had every right to freak out."

"I ran away without even giving Nick a chance," Charlotte said miserably. "You didn't want me to go, and Gran told me I needed to talk with him, but I wouldn't. Just think of how differently our lives might have been if I'd listened."

Becca reached over and patted Charlotte's hand. "Things might have been different, Lottie," she told her, "but different isn't always better. Your gran would have said, 'There's no use crying over spilled milk,' and she'd be right. Leave the past in the past and focus on the future. So, when is the wedding?"

Charlotte laughed so hard that she almost wet her pants! "Slow down Mrs. Tyler," Charlotte said. "We're still trying to learn how to get along as grown-ups, marriage is the last thing on our minds."

Becca had a dreamy look on her face, but just replied, "Whatever you say, Sweetie, whatever you say."

Chapter 63

Now

The pampering was wonderful, and both Charlotte and Becca agreed they hadn't had a better day together in years. No men, kids, or drama entered their room at the spa, and it felt like old times! They were about to have their eyebrows and legs waxed when the attendant asked if either one of them was interested in a Brazilian wax. Charlotte looked at Becca, and together they shook their heads.

While the esthetician warmed the wax, and got everything ready, Charlotte whispered to Becca, "Have you ever thought about having a Brazilian?"

"Let's put it this way," Becca replied. "I'm married to a pediatrician, and he told me early on that the last thing he wanted was for his wife to look like a prepubescent girl. Jared not only finds it unattractive, but he says it isn't healthy either. How about you?"

Charlotte let out the breath she'd been holding in, thankful she wasn't the only woman on the planet who had no interesting in waxing her privates. "I used to wonder about it but never really had the inclination. Then, when Nick and I got together, I worried that he might be used to such extremes, but he told me it turned him on how natural I was, and that was all I needed to hear."

"It sounds really painful to me anyway," Becca added. "I go through enough pain in that area just pushing out babies." Realizing what she'd said, Becca looked over at Charlotte and saw the look of panic on her face.

"I'm so sorry, Charlotte, please forget I said that. Once you hold that baby in your arms for the first time, you'll forget all about labor." Becca smiled, hoping she'd been convincing. Thankfully the esthetician was ready for them, and they both forgot about labor pains as other parts of their bodies were soon feeling the burn of hair removal!

After the waxing was a soothing herbal rub, and then on to mani pedis. By the end of the day, both women were almost limp with relaxation and ready for a nap. "I'm so exhausted," Charlotte told Becca with a big yawn. "Who would think a day of being treated like a queen would be so tiring?"

"I'm with you there, Sister, but you still have to drive us home." Becca reminded her.

"Would it be awful if I called Nick to see if Pop or Noah could pick us up? I don't think he's been cleared to drive or I would just ask him," Charlotte asked, trying to suppress another yawn.

"What about your car? Surely you don't want to leave it here overnight?" Becca answered.

"I'm going to call him and see if Noah and Pop are around, and if so, they can come together and one of them can drive my car back. I honestly don't think I can be trusted to get us home safely."

Nick was relieved Charlotte had called him, rather than taking a chance driving when she was so tired and said they would be there in about twenty minutes. Accepting bottles of water from the receptionist, Charlotte and Becca left nice tips for their attendants, and walked across the street to the beach to wait for their ride.

"Since we have a few minutes I'm going to call Mom and check on the kids," Becca told Charlotte. With a limp nod, about all that she could muster, Charlotte sat down on a bench, sipping her water and enjoying the rolling waves on the Gulf of Mexico.

Chapter 64

Now

"How would you feel about a slumber party tonight?" Becca asked Charlotte after ending the call with her mom. "Big girls only, of course, and the way I feel right now, I think slumber is just what I have in mind."

"I'd love it, but what about your kiddos? Are you up for a night away from them?" Charlotte questioned.

"Mom and Dad are taking them to the Mote Aquarium and then to The Old Salty Dog for dinner. JD's been begging to go there ever since we saw it on the Food Network, and there's no bigger sucker than my dad when it comes to those kids. They'll fall asleep on the way home, so we might as well extend our day. What do you say?" Becca asked again. "Are we up for a girl's night, or not?"

Charlotte laughed. "Girls' night it is!" she exclaimed, "only without wine it's going to be a little calmer than normal."

"You might as well get over that craving for adult beverages, Lottie Lou, because between the pregnancy, and the nursing, you won't be having any fermented drinks for years!" Becca gave Charlotte a sly smile and took a gulp of her water. "Get used to it, Sweetie, you're in mommy mode now."

Before she could respond, Charlotte looked up and saw Nick and Noah walking towards her and Becca. "Where's Pop?" she questioned. "We need him to drive back my car."

"He had a boat come in for fuel, so Noah and I are here to be your chauffeurs. Before you get all mother henish on me," Nick said with a wink, "it's fine for me to drive short distances."

Charlotte wasn't convinced, but she wasn't up for an argument, so she was walking to Nick's Jeep, just as Becca spoke-up.

"Nick and I haven't had any time to catch up," Becca told the group. "Why don't I ride with him, and you can ride back with Noah in your car, Lottie?"

Nick groaned, and Charlotte looked at him as if to say, "Help," but he just shrugged his shoulders and let Becca climb into his Jeep. After such a perfect day, this is not at all what Charlotte wanted, but she knew when Becca had her mind set on something there was no changing it.

Settling in the passenger seat of her beloved Gran Prix, Charlotte closed her eyes, hoping Noah would see how sleepy she was and not talk. Unfortunately, that was not to be!

"So, I hear you're going to make me an Uncle," Noah said before they had even pulled out of the parking lot.

Shit! Shit! Shit! Charlotte said to herself. I knew this whole ride idea was going to bite me in the ass! But to Noah she calmly asked, "How do you feel about that?"

Noah smiled at her, but it wasn't that crazy Hollywood smile she was used to. "You know I told you I always knew you were Nick's girl, and I meant that, but I guess somewhere deep inside was a fantasy that someday you'd realize I was the guy for you, and we'd sail off in the sunset together. Hearing about the baby was like locking the door on a dream, but hey, it's one that needed to be locked away anyway."

Charlotte couldn't keep the tears at bay. "I don't know what to say, Noah," she cried. "Hurting you is the last thing I would ever want to do, but Nick's always been the one for me. Please tell me you understand."

"Dry your eyes, Shortcake. It's just that you're sitting there all pink and pretty, with a soft glow on your face, and your nails all painted, and it stabbed at my heart a little bit. But honestly, this just may have been the best thing for me, because now I know I have to move on. Nick is so happy Lottie, and he deserves that; you both do." This time when Noah smiled at her it was full-on Hollywood, but it didn't make Charlotte's heart hurt any less.

Chapter 65

Now

By the time they all arrived back at Charlotte's cottage, she was dead on her feet and an emotional wreck. She played with her locket and silently talked with her gran all the way home after Noah's revelation, and if she ever needed a glass of wine, it was now!

Pulling in behind them, Becca climbed out of Nick's Jeep and addressed the foursome. "Nick and I talked on the way over, and after we gals take a nap, we're going to meet back up around seven at the Cortez Kitchen. I haven't had good cheese grits in ages." Without stopping for air Becca added, "Pop's coming too of course."

Charlotte just wanted to climb into bed and pull the covers over her head, but when Noah said, "Sounds like a plan to me," she knew there was no getting out of it.

Nick came around to where Charlotte was standing and looked straight into her eyes. "I was hoping your spa day would help you relax, but that's not the vibe I'm picking up on. What's going on?"

There was no way she could talk about this now, not with Noah standing just a few feet away, so instead she smiled and told him a little white lie. "It was amazing Nick, and I can't thank you enough for the wonderful indulgence you gave us, but I'm so relaxed that I'm almost comatose. Let us go in and get a couple of hours sleep, and I'll be good as new by seven."

Trying her best not to let him have time to read her face, she gave him a quick peck on the cheek and headed up the walk to her door. She could hear Nick and Becca talking, but she didn't care. If she couldn't have wine at least she could have juice, so she poured herself a big glass and tumbled into bed. Laying there waiting for Becca to come in,

Charlotte closed her eyes and was sound asleep before her friend climbed in beside her.

Charlotte couldn't remember what she'd been dreaming about, but whatever it was brought her from sound asleep to wide awake in less than a minute. Trying to steady her breathing, she looked over at the sleeping form beside her and let out a long sigh when she realized it was Becca. Picking up her phone she saw that it was five forty-five, and knew she needed to get in the shower now or they'd be late for their dinner date.

Leaving Becca to sleep for a little longer, Charlotte turned on her fancy shower and let the soothing water bring her back to life. Her muscles were sore from the deep tissue massage, but the wonderful streams of hot water, combined with her nap, were just what she needed to feel normal again. Stepping out of the shower she grabbed a big, fluffy towel and was just starting to dry off when she heard Becca call to her.

"Are you decent, Lottie?" Becca asked, "because I've really got to pee. This baby is definitely a kicker, and right now it's kicking me in the bladder!"

Charlotte was laughing as she exited the bathroom, just in time for Becca to race past her. "You just wait smarty pants," Becca called as she plopped down on the toilet. "Your time's coming."

Charlotte realized while Becca was in the shower that she wouldn't have any clean clothes to put on, and it posed a dilemma. Becca was a good five inches shorter than she was, plus her tummy was more than a bump; she was full-on pregnant! Looking through her drawers and closet, Charlotte was able to come up with a pair of yoga pants that hit her at the knee, but would be ankle length on Becca, plus a bright red tunic style T-shirt she had never worn because the color wasn't right with her hair. Undies were a real issue, but finding a pair of lowcut boy shorts, she laid them out, hoping they would fit under Becca's belly.

"You're the best friend a girl could ask for," Becca hollered out from the bathroom when she eyed the clothes. "Who would think clean underwear would be such a lifesaver for us, but I guess it means my mom was right, you need to be prepared for any situation."

168

Becca stepped out of the bathroom fully dressed and looking cute as a button. "You might as well keep the outfit," Charlotte told her friend. "The shirt was a gift from my mom, who obviously doesn't remember the color of my hair, and you may need the pants again this week. But what am I going to wear? I tried on my skinny jeans while you were dressing and the button won't close. I really love this baby, but I'm not pleased at how fast its popping out!"

"I'm going to share a mommy trick with you for your pants," Becca said, grabbing a stretched-out ponytail holder from Charlotte's dresser. "Put your jeans back on and let me show you how to keep wearing your favorite pants for a little while longer."

Charlotte pulled the jeans up, and Becca wrapped the elastic band around the button of the jeans, through the buttonhole, and back around the button, giving Charlotte just the extra room that she needed. "See," she said with a grin, "You can wear these puppies for at least another couple of weeks! But Charlotte, is there any chance you're having twins? That bump of yours seems a little rounder than I would have thought."

Charlotte turned an unattractive shade of puce and flopped on her bed. "There had better not be," she said with force. "I know that Maya has twins, but I've never thought to ask Nick if they run in his family. To be honest, he probably doesn't even know. *"Shit, shit, shit!"* she said out loud. "Being an unwed mother is going to be bad enough, but an unwed mother with twins, unfreaking believable!"

"Have you had an ultrasound yet?" Becca questioned. "That should tell you for sure." Charlotte shook her head. "Not until my next appointment, and that's still a few weeks away. This was supposed to be our big day of pampering, and it's all just gone to hell! Damn Nick Greyson and his and super-strong sperm. Noah's hurting, I feel fat, and it's all Nick's fault!"

Becca covered her mouth to keep from laughing at her friend. "I don't know what to tell you, Sweetie, but I'm confident Nick had help making this baby. And as for Noah, you can tell me what's going on with him during our ride to the Cortez Kitchen. I'm pretty sure a grouper sandwich and a plate of their onion rings will make everything better, and if we don't get going, we're going to be more than fashionably late."

Charlotte grabbed her keys and her pink Coach clutch and headed out the door with Becca. She knew food was not the answer to her problems, but damn if a grouper sandwich didn't sound good!

Chapter 66
Now

Charlotte and Becca arrived at the Cortez Kitchen a few minutes after seven, the revelation from Noah out in the open and discussed. They found the Greyson men were sitting at a table laughing, beers in front of Pop and Noah, and a Coke in front of Nick, but the minute he saw Charlotte, Nick was on his feet and moving her way.

"How was your nap?" he asked, remembering how indignant he had become a couple of weeks earlier when she had asked him the same question.

"Wonderful and exactly what I needed," Charlotte answered with a smile.

Embracing her cautiously, as if she was a piece of china, Nick asked, "Are we okay?"

Charlotte looked up at his deep blue eyes and saw worry there. How could she tell him about her conversation with his brother without ruining the evening or causing trouble between the two of them? She knew that she couldn't do anything to cause any more hurt for the Greyson family, so she went with door number two!

"Let me ask you this question first," Charlotte answered him. "Do twins run in your family?"

"I have no idea," Nick responded. "Why are you even asking me that?"

Taking his hand, she gently pressed it against her stomach and let him feel her baby bump. "Because my clothes are already getting tight, and I'm worried that Babycakes might have a teammate in there with him, and if you got me pregnant with twins, Nick Greyson, I'm going to be really pissed off!"

Nick couldn't stop laughing, and that did piss her off! "I don't see what's so funny?" she spat at him. "This is serious!"

Getting his laughing under control, Nick answered her. "Is the concern about twins because of Nikki and Steffi? Because that DNA belongs all to Dimitri. He's a twin, and his dad is a twin, so I don't think I can be held responsible for what goes on with the Maras family, do you? My parents are both only children, so if there were ever twins, it was back a few generations."

Suddenly Charlotte remembered that they were in a public place and looked up to see Pop and Becca, plus a few of the other diners, looking their way. With a meek smile on her face she led Nick to their table and without missing a beat asked Pop, "So how was your day?"

They were half way through grouper sandwiches, cheese grits, and onion rings when Noah turned his attention to Becca. "I've got to say Sister Rebecca Rose, you turned into one mighty fine-looking woman. Why is it you and I never hooked up?"

"Well to begin with," Becca chuckled, "calling me Sister makes me realize you remembered my desire to be a Nun, which is pretty much why I didn't hook up, as you so gallantly call it, with anyone. Plus, Noah Greyson, you were more like a brother to me than boyfriend material, and you were hooking up with any girl in a three-county radius who would have you."

Noah tried to look sheepish, but he couldn't. "So, what was it about the good Doctor Tyler that changed your mind?" he asked her.

Becca's eyes got soft when she thought about the first time she had met Jared Tyler. "Because when I looked up at him, I saw my future, and that future was with him."

The table was quiet for a moment, because how do you respond to a statement like that? Finally, Nick broke the silence by lifting his can of Coke and saying, "To the future, may we all find our happily ever after." With that he took Charlotte's hand in his, and as he looked into her glass green eyes, he knew he had found his.

Chapter 67

Now

Early the morning after their sleepover Becca was up and ready to head back to her mom's, anxious to see her towheaded babies. Charlotte looked at her friend in awe, wondering how she stayed so calm being a mom and a doctor's wife, and she hoped she would learn a thing or two before her own child was born.

Becca's mom met them at the front door, holding Baby Charlotte, who immediately reached for Becca the minute she saw her. "Good morning beautiful," Becca whispered as she nuzzled her sleepy daughter. "Did you have a good time with Grampy and Grammy?"

Lolly, as she was affectionately called, nodded, and snuggled down in her mother's arms.

"We're having a cookout around four o'clock," Mrs. Huddleston told Charlotte. "We'd love it if you and Nick would join us. His dad too, if he's available."

Charlotte smiled, remembering what a warm and caring woman Becca's mom was. "It sounds great, but I need to check with them and get back with you. Is that okay?"

"It's perfect!" beamed Becca's mom. "You girls can talk later and let me know." She held out her arms to take Lolly back in with her, but with her thumb in her mouth, and her mother's arms around her, it was obvious that Charlotte Tyler was not about to leave her mommy's side.

"Thanks for a wonderful get-a-way, Lottie," Becca said, trying to hold her daughter and hug her friend all at the same time. "I really enjoyed spending time with Nick and Noah last night, although I hate all the issues you and Noah have had. Hopefully they'll die down soon, and of course, anytime I'm with you is special." With a kiss to

Charlotte's cheek, Becca took her contented daughter and went inside to greet the rest of her brood.

The week with Becca and her kids went by quickly, with Charlotte managing to find time to get her new client's financial records in order and finding time to play on the beach with the three Tyler kids. Nick joined them a couple of times, and even let JD bury him in sand. It was obvious to both Charlotte and Becca that Nick Greyson was going to be every bit as great a father as Pop was.

On Thursday afternoon, Charlotte and Nick took all three kids to her house while Becca drove to Sarasota to pick-up Jared. They offered to keep them all night so Becca and Jared could spend some time alone, but Jared had missed his family, and wanted them all together when he got home.

"What do you think, Charlotte?" Nick asked her with a wink. "Are you up for three kids?"

"I'm pretty sure we had this talk before, and my answer hasn't changed. Let's see how things go with this baby, and maybe someday, we can discuss having more." Nick nodded, but with Anna curled up in his lap, and JD all but hanging off of him, it was pretty easy for Charlotte to see Nick Greyson was a natural where kids were concerned. The problem was, their baby wasn't planned, and the last thing she wanted was to pop out Greyson babies when there was no official commitment between them.

As soon as Lolly woke up from her nap, Nick and Charlotte guided the kids to the trolley, and a special trip to Two Scoops. "Your mom and your Aunt TT and I used to come here all the time when we were growing up," Nick told them, holding Lolly safely in his arms. "There's nothing like a trolley ride and an ice cream cone on a hot afternoon."

By the time Becca and Jared were headed home from the airport, the three Tylers were ready to see their daddy, and Nick and Charlotte knew they had to give them up, even though they hated to. When Jared stepped out of the car, the kids ran to him, and he hugged and kissed them as if he had been gone for months. After quickly introducing Jared to Nick, Charlotte said she would see her friends tomorrow night at the party, and she and Nick turned to go back into her house. They were almost at the door when JD came running their way and threw himself in Nick's arms.

"Now that you're Aunt TT's boyfriend, we'll see you a lot, right?" JD asked, looking up at Nick.

"You bet you will, Slugger," Nick said, ruffling JD's blond hair. "You just try to keep me away."

Satisfied, JD ran back to his family and climbed into the back seat of the car. Becca blew Charlotte a kiss and mouthed, "I love you," and the Tylers were off.

Chapter 68

Now

"What a week!" Charlotte exclaimed when they got back inside. "I loved having Becca and the kids so close, and I actually got some work done, too, but I feel like I've been neglecting you. Are you feeling okay?"

Nick pulled her in close and smiled. "I'm doing great, Charlotte, you don't have to worry about me. I loved spending time with Becca and her kids, as well, and it's great having Noah home, but I've really missed you. Some things happened this week that I haven't been able to tell you about, and I'm hoping this weekend we can catch up."

"What's happened, Nick?" Charlotte asked with concern in her voice. "Why can't you tell me now?"

"I can," he replied with a chuckle. "I'm just not going to. And before you pout, the answer is still no, and anyway, we need to drive down to Ginny's & Jane E's to get some fancy wine glasses for the party tomorrow. Maya called and they're holding them for her, but we need to get there before they close at five."

"You're mean," Charlotte answered like a petulant child, but she allowed Nick to direct her to her car without any more fuss.

Ginny's & Jane E's was just a few miles away on Gulf Drive, and its eclectic atmosphere never failed to charm Charlotte. She loved all the refurbished Florida style décor, plus in the back was a lunchroom of sorts, and books! Lots of books. The wine glasses Maya ordered had been hand painted by a local artist especially for Stavros, and Nick and Charlotte were struck by their beauty.

On their way home, Charlotte took a detour and pulled up behind Mrs. Danvers's bungalow. "I want you to meet a friend of mine," she told Nick, and taking his hand, she led him around front.

"Mrs. D., it's me Charlotte," she called as she knocked on the door. "I don't have contraband, but I do have someone important I want to introduce you to."

Mrs. Danvers smiled as she let Nick and Charlotte inside. "Why you're that FBI man I saw on TV, aren't you?" she asked first thing. Nick was starting to worry that coming here might not have been a good thing when Mrs. Danvers spoke again.

"It was a wonderful thing you did for Anna Maria, young man. I'm just sorry for all the backlash it caused." Looking at Charlotte, Mrs. D. continued, "I can tell a keeper when I see one, Charlotte, and this one's a keeper. Why, he even reminds me of my Leo."

Charlotte blushed, especially when Nick took her hand, but secretly she was thrilled to have her good friend's blessing. She thought Nick was a keeper, too, and this time she wasn't going to let him go!

Chapter 69

Now

On Friday morning, Charlotte woke up alone but full of excitement. Nick had decided he needed to stay at the marina while Noah was home which allowed Charlotte time to fawn over her new purchases in private. She hadn't dressed up to go out since before Nick came back to the island, but she was making up for it now!

Opening her closet, she pulled out the Tadashi Shoji sleeveless, floral chiffon handkerchief dress she had ordered from Neiman Marcus as soon as she got home from Maya's the week before. The fact that it had a light blue background, Nick's favorite color, and she was going to wear it to his thank you dinner, sealed the deal. And of course, she had to order the Cleva Metallic Strappy Ankle-Wrap sandals from Manolo Blahnik to go with it! Neiman's had a special gift card offer on both items, so it was practically like getting them for free, or at least, that's what she told herself.

Sinking down on her bed, her beautiful dress in her hands, Charlotte wondered what Nick would think of her designer clothes spending habit. After all, it wasn't like she was spending his money, but she did know a conversation about their finances was probably in order. For now, she was going to luxuriate in the way fancy clothes made her feel, and then she wondered, do designers make maternity clothes?

After a run on the beach and a few hours spent looking over the records on Tony Neel's computer, Charlotte was ready for a light lunch and an afternoon nap. Finding some smoked gouda cheese and fruit in the refrigerator she grabbed a box of Triscuits and a glass of ice tea and took her food to the lanai.

It had been so long since she had relaxed in her little enclosed sanctuary she had forgotten how had peaceful it was. Making a sandwich out of crackers, cheese, and a piece of cantaloupe, she popped it in her mouth and savored the mix of flavors. "I'm so glad we're past the whole morning sickness thing, Babycakes," Charlotte said as she rubbed her tummy. "Your mommy has a love/hate relationship with food, I admit, but once I've decided to eat it, I expect it to stay down."

After a few more little sandwiches and a large glass of iced tea, Charlotte headed for her bedroom and a long nap. She had no idea how long the party would last tonight, and she didn't want to ruin it for Nick by nodding off in front of his friends.

Chapter 70

Now

After a glorious afternoon nap wrapped in a soft, five-hundred-thread-count sheet, dreaming of Nick, Charlotte woke up invigorated and ready to start her toilette for the evening's festivities! Maya hadn't allowed her to help in any way. All Charlotte knew was the party room of Stavros' was where the celebration was being held, and several people had been invited. Defining several scared her a little, but at least Jared and Becca would be there so she'd have someone to hang out with while Nick was schmoozing with the crowd.

Just as she was thinking about getting into the shower Nick called, and all thoughts about exfoliating and deep conditioning took a back seat. "Hey gorgeous," he said seductively, "I can't wait to see you. Have you enjoyed your day on your own?"

Charlotte wasn't sure if he wanted her to say she missed him, or she had liked the solitude of the day, so she compromised. "I got a lot done, and I took a long nap, but of course having you next to me would have made it better." There, wasn't that straight out of Relationship 101?

Nick groaned. "And I would have liked to have been there, but I had a productive day as well, so now we can just concentrate on tonight, right?"

"Right," Charlotte said with a smile, and there was no compromise in the way her face lit up. "So, what time do I need to pick the guest of honor up?"

"I hate that I can't drive long distances yet," Nick grumbled. "I have us a chauffeur, actually a pair of them. Becca called this morning and asked if we wanted to ride with them. She thought it might give

Jared and me a chance to get to know each other before we're in a room full of people. What do you think?"

"I think it sounds perfect," Charlotte all but purred. Now she could enjoy the evening without the stress of driving in her new shoes! "What time will they pick me up?"

"The plan is for them to get me at five and then we'll swing by your house. I know it's closer to get you first and then come to the marina, but I want to pick my girl up at the front door for our evening out."

Charlotte didn't think her smile could get any bigger, but damned if it didn't. "You're so gallant, Nick Greyson; who knew?"

"My dad raised me right, Lottie, you know that."

Charlotte noticed that Nick was using "Lottie" a little more than he had been, but she wasn't going to mention it today. Lots of people still called her Lottie, and she was fine with it, but with Nick she needed to make sure it was Charlotte he wanted, and not the girl from his youth.

"I'll be waiting with bells on," Charlotte teased.

Nick replied, "Only bells? That's the image I'll keep in my head for the next couple of hours. You're the love of my life, Charlotte Luce, I'll see you soon." With those parting words, Nick hung up.

Chapter 71

Now

Charlotte luxuriated in the hot water, letting it rain down over her head and body like she was standing under a waterfall. Her fancy shower, as Nick called it, was one of the first investments she had made when she moved into her little cottage on the beach, and she felt it was worth every penny.

Rubbing a generous dollop of Moroccanoil shampoo in her hands, Charlotte began the long process of washing and conditioning her thick, curly locks. Jenn, her stylist at Shine Salon, had recommended it for her hair type, and so far, Charlotte had to agree, it was amazing! After a double washing and thorough rinsing, she applied the Moroccanoil conditioner and clipped her hair up to allow it to work it's magic while she took care of the rest of her body.

Grabbing her Philosophy Living Grace hot salt scrub Charlotte gave her skin a good exfoliation and loved how soft and silky she felt after using it. Her legs were still smooth from the waxing at the Sea-renity Spa on Saturday, but just to be on the safe side, she lightly ran a razor over them before shaving under her arms. After that it was time to rinse everything off and get out of the shower. Reaching for a couple of her thick, Egyptian cotton towels, Charlotte wrapped one around her head and the other around her body. Feeling squeaky clean, she grabbed the jar of Living Grace body lotion and slathered it over every inch of her skin.

While she combed out her hair, Charlotte glanced at the award sitting on her dresser she won from Olde Florida Bank. For the first time it hit her how much she missed her job there, as well as the team she had worked with. She was thankful she had been able to be at the hospital while Nick was so critical, and she knew she was blessed to have found the small accounting job with the AMI small business owners, but her relationship with Olde Florida was more than a job. It had been her life, and it was a life she knew she had lost.

"Get a grip, girl," she told herself. "Now is not the time to feel sorry for yourself! This night is all about Nick."

Her hair tangle free, she rubbed in lots of Moroccanoil Curl Defining Cream and then got out her hair dryer and diffuser. Charlotte knew her hair would dry curly, but that was all part of her plan because she had seen a hairstyle in a magazine that showed the model with an elegant curly updo, and that was her goal for the evening.

Hair and body taken care of, Charlotte looked over her skimpy supply of make-up and tried to decide how to best utilize it. Wanting more than her normal swipe of blush, mascara, and lip gloss, she applied Josie Maran tinted moisturizer over her entire face to give herself a golden glow. Next came a swipe of *ooh la lift* in the corners of her eyes and below her brows, followed by Mally cream eyeshadow in both Shimmering Lilac and Champagne. Finally, her usual swipe of mascara and blush, and she was done.

Charlotte looked at the woman in the mirror and had trouble recognizing herself. Feeling like a femme fatale she said out loud, "Let's see what kind of self-defense Special Agent Greyson has against this!"

It was finally time to get dressed and Charlotte was nervous with excitement. She and Nick had never gone out on a fancy date together, but more importantly, she wanted to make a good impression on his friends and not let him down. She knew he would say that wasn't possible, but women looked at things from a different perspective. Besides, only a few people knew she was pregnant so the fit and the style of her dress was more important than ever.

Silvery sandals tied around her ankles and wispy billows of chiffon floating from her waist, Charlotte felt like a princess. The only things left to do were spritzing herself with the new O De Lancôme she had purchased especially for tonight and applying her Josie Maran Lip Sting Plumping Butter that almost matched the color of her mani pedi,

183

and she was done. Just as she was about to grab her evening bag, she heard Nick knock and walk on in.

"If you look anything as good as you smell," he said as he waited for her to appear, "we may not make it out of here."

Stepping out of her bedroom, Charlotte looked at Nick for a reaction. When he didn't speak, she asked him with a shaky voice, "You don't like it?"

"Like doesn't even begin to describe how you look or how I'm feeling right now," Nick replied hoarsely. "You look like every man's fantasy, and I can't believe you're mine."

With those words, she stepped into his arms and savored the taste of his kiss and the strength of his embrace. When he moved his hands up her back and found her soft, smooth skin, he swore. "Holy fuck. How am I supposed to let you waltz around all night half naked in a room full of men? Don't you have a sweater or something you can put on?"

It was all Charlotte could do to keep from laughing at him, so she slipped her arms around his waist and brought her mouth back to his. That was all the distraction he needed, because the next thing she knew his hands were moving over her breasts, and she was moaning into his mouth.

"I want you so badly," Nick whispered in her ear. "How much longer are you going to make me wait?"

"If our carriage doesn't turn into a pumpkin at midnight, how about after the party?" Charlotte said in her most sultry voice.

Nick sighed and nodded his head in relief as he pulled himself back from her. "I can wait a few more hours," he told her, "but I'm going to embarrass us both if we don't stop now."

Just then Charlotte heard the honk of the car in her driveway and knew they had been saved by the proverbial bell. Walking out the door hand in hand, they were greeted by Becca, who announced as she handed Nick a tissue, "That shade of lipstick isn't right for you Greyson. With your coloring, you need something a little darker."

Nick took the tissue from Becca, wiped off his mouth and handed it back to her without a word. And with that, he ushered Charlotte into the backseat of the waiting car.

Chapter 72

Now

Nick and Jared chatted like old friends during the trip to Tarpon Springs, but Nick kept his hand firmly on Charlotte's knee the whole time. A couple of times he even tried to move his hand higher up, and despite not wanting to, Charlotte always moved it back down.

"This is a pretty sweet ride," Nick said to Jared, as he looked over the posh interior of the Lincoln Town Car. "I drive a Jeep, so this is like being in a limo."

Jared chuckled before responding. "Becca and I both drive Toyotas, so it's a big step up for us, as well, but her dad really wanted this night to be special, so he insisted we take his Lincoln. I've got to say I could get used to this, but it might be hard to explain on the days I work at the Free Clinic."

They all agreed that Jared's Prius was probably the best choice for him, but the smooth ride of the Town Car was pretty much perfect for this night.

"So, what kind of stories can you tell me from when you and these ladies were kids?" Jared quizzed Nick. "I've probably heard all the main ones, but surely you know something about my wife that I don't."

"We have less than an hour's ride left and that's not near enough time to tell you about the Bobbsey Twins," Nick laughed. "The next time we're together I can tell you plenty." Becca gave Jared a playful smack on his arm, and Charlotte rolled her eyes.

"Boys!" they said in unison, but Charlotte was thrilled Jared and Nick seemed to be getting along. After her break-up with Ryan, she'd kept her dates away from Jared, because she knew they would never meet his high standards. To be honest, those dates hadn't met her standards either, and although she had introduced Peter to Becca, she should have known right away he wasn't the one for her.

Everyone was quiet the last few minutes of the drive, and Charlotte used them to look over the handsome man sitting beside her. Nick had always had something special, even as a boy, but now he was hands down the most gorgeous looking man she had ever seen. Dressed up in a suit and tie, his hair freshly cut and perfectly placed, she was pretty certain he could have been a model with Miss Harper if he'd wanted to. What a pair they would have made on the pages of a fashion magazine, but instead he was in the backseat of a car with her. Gran's locket and a pair of diamond earrings were the only jewelry she wore. Her fingers automatically caressed the locket as she shared her feelings with her grandmother.

"Hi Gran," Charlotte said without uttering a word. "Can you believe the man Nick has grown-up to be? He's so handsome and kind, and he loves me, Gran. Me, chubby awkward Lottie Luce. Ashley was wrong about me, Gran, because I was never a loser; I'm a winner and it's you and Nick who made me realize it. I love you, Gran, and I'll never stop missing you."

Jared pulled into the parking lot of Stavros and turned off the car, but Nick made no move to get out. Sensing he needed a minute, Jared opened Becca's door and the two of them headed into the restaurant.

"Nick?" Charlotte questioned. "What's the matter?" Taking his hands in hers, she realized he was trembling, and it scared her to death. "I'm going to get Jared," she cried, but Nick held her back.

"I don't need a doctor, Charlotte," he told her with a weak smile. "Just a little nervous now that this night is finally here."

"I don't understand," she implored. "These people are your friends and family; what's there to be nervous about?"

"Nothing," he said with a genuine smile this time. "Come on, I want to show off my lovely lady."

Helping her from the car, Nick held on to Charlotte's hand as they walked up the lighted path to Stavros. Just before he opened the door he turned to her and said, "Promise me you'll never run away from me again, Charlotte. Promise me, okay?"

"I don't know what's going on with you, Nick Greyson, but my heart is pounding out of my chest I'm so afraid, and I'm pretty certain that isn't good for your child." Charlotte was almost in tears at this point, which made Nick feel like a jerk.

"Everything is fine, I promise," Nick tried to sooth her. "I'm just having a little stage fright, I guess."

Together they stepped inside and into the paradise that Maya had turned Stavros into, and once again, Nick was calm and confident.

Chapter 73

Now

"You're here!" cried Maya, as she hugged her brother tight. "When Becca and Jared came in without you, I was afraid you had cold feet."

Nick just looked at his sister and shook his head. "It's been awhile since I've been to a fancy gathering like this," he told her. "I just needed a minute."

Maya seemed to understand and turned her attention on Charlotte. "You look so beautiful, Lottie," Maya gushed. "In that dress, no one can even tell you're pregnant. And congratulations by the way, Dimi and I are thrilled for you both." Putting her arms around Charlotte, Maya whispered in her ear, "We haven't told the twins yet though, because those little pitchers have big ears and big mouths!"

Charlotte blushed, realizing this was the first time she had seen Maya and Dimi since Nick had shared their news, but she was thankful that the girls didn't know yet. This was Nick's night, and they had agreed her pregnancy would not be a topic for conversation.

"Thanks, Maya," Charlotte told Nick's sister, "on both counts."

Linking herself between Nick and Charlotte, Maya escorted them into the party room and the wonder she had turned the restaurant into. "Well, what do you think?" she quizzed. "It looks pretty good, if I do say so myself."

Just then Dimi came into the room, offering a handshake to Nick and a soft hug and kiss to Charlotte. "My wife's outdone herself, don't you agree?" Dimi asked. "I may be prejudice, but she's the best party planner in the state."

"It's perfect, Sis," Nick said, kissing his sister on the top of her head. "I can't thank you enough for everything."

Soon Pop and Noah arrived, bringing with them a special surprise for Charlotte. "Shelly!" she squealed when her friend walked in. "You told me you had to work all weekend."

"It was just one little fib, Charlotte, but I couldn't resist when Nicholas suggested it." Shelly told her.

"Nicholas, huh?" Charlotte teased, but she could see in Shelly's eyes the importance of that statement. "Well, why don't you and I go find Becca so I can introduce my newest friend to my oldest friend. And then maybe you can give us both the 911 on Nicholas."

Guests started to filter in and Charlotte couldn't believe how many people were there. Both Dr. Copeland and Dr. Rivers had arrived, bringing with them a spouse or a date, and she looked up just in time to see Director James, of the Tampa FBI field office, walk in with a stunning brunette. She was just contemplating whether she should go talk with them or not when in walked two of the people from her team at Olde Florida Bank.

Charlotte felt as if she couldn't breathe as she watched Dan and Pam walk her way. "Oh, my gosh," she cried, "it's so good to see you!" With hugs all around and promises to talk later in the evening, Charlotte went to Nick, who was motioning her his way.

"Maya says we need to take our seats so the servers can start the first course. I'm not sure what all we're having, but knowing my sister, it's going to be a lot of food."

Sitting at the head table with Nick, Charlotte felt very much on display, and without the benefit of a glass of wine, also very nervous. He held her hand between courses and was very attentive, but every time she looked up, it felt as if everyone was staring her way.

After a dessert of Dimi's fabulous chocolate baklava, which Charlotte was too nervous to eat, Maya whispered in Nick's ear that it was time for him to speak. In front of everyone he kissed her hand and pushed away from the table.

"I can't begin to tell you how much it means to me to have you all here tonight. This is a very special occasion, and if it weren't for most of you, I might not be here to even say thank you. Dr. Copeland and Dr. Rivers, you gave me the best medical care I could have asked for.

Shelly, you and your staff made sure I was always surrounded by kind and caring hands, and my family made sure I was never alone. The thoughts and prayers of so many of you put me in the hands of the one true healer, and I wish I had a stronger word than thank you to give." Nick took a drink of his water and let out a deep breath before continuing.

"I'm standing here today because so many people were in my corner, but the one person who truly gave me the will to come out of the darkness was Charlotte." Hearing her name, Charlotte looked at Nick in disbelief, as he looked down on her.

"Charlotte, you talked to me, and soothed me, and told me that you loved me, and there was no way in hell I was going to die in that hospital bed after that. I waited over twelve years to hear you say those words, and now I need to say some words to you. Our friend Becca reminded me this week that you don't like surprises, but I'm praying that you'll forgive me for this one."

Charlotte felt the color coming up on her face as she wondered what Nick might say, and then, two things happened at once. From out of the shadows of the room her mom appeared, and beside her, Nick got down on one knee.

Taking her hand, Nick spoke. "Charlotte Luce, I've loved you since I was a boy. You were my friend and my confidant, and the one person who always made me feel whole, and you're still that person today. I lost you once, well actually I lost you twice, and I don't ever want to spend another day without you by my side. Lottie, Charlotte, what we have together is forever and I want the world to know it." Nick opened a small, white velvet box, and the tears started to fall as Charlotte stared at the square cut, aquamarine ring with channel set diamonds that had belonged to Gran. "Marry me Charlotte," was all that he said.

"Mom?" she whispered, her voice quivering and soft, and when she closed her eyes she saw the face of her gran, and the memories came tumbling back.

Chapter 74

Then

"We need to run some errands in town this morning, Lottie," Gran told her, "and we'll have lunch at the Chicken and Steak. I'm in the mood for a cheeseburger and a milkshake."

Lottie laughed because the Chicken and Steak was her favorite restaurant in Martinsville, and Gran always took her there at least once while she was visiting. Despite her new hair-do and contacts, and her efforts to lose a few pounds, the peanut butter milkshakes were to die for, and she wasn't about to turn one down!

After leaving a pair of shoes at the Bootery for a heel replacement, and stopping by the Quilt Rack for some material, Gran ushered Lottie into the Martinsville Savings Bank. Lottie was always amazed at how everyone in town not only knew her gran, but also knew all about her, but it didn't stop Gran from introducing her to everyone she talked with.

"This is my granddaughter, Lottie Luce, from Florida." Gran told the bank manager. "She's visiting with me for the whole month." Gran's smile showed her pride as she talked about Lottie and her accomplishments in school, but all Lottie could do was blush. Being the center of attention was definitely outside of her comfort level.

Finally, everyone had met Lottie and talked with Gran, and Gran asked to be let into her safety deposit box. Lottie felt very important as she was asked to sign the access card as a guest, and then she and Gran were led to a little room next to the vault that the attendant called the coupon room.

Gran took a seat at the little table and motioned for Lottie to pull up the extra chair and join her. Lottie had never been this far inside a bank before and doubted if her mom had anything important enough to keep in a locked-up box in a bank vault. This new adventure was very exciting!

Gran looked through some papers and from the back of the box she pulled out a beautiful, white velvet box. Lottie was used to Gran being strong and stoic, and she was a little uncertain what to do when she saw tears forming in Gran's eyes. But when Gran opened the box she smiled as she told Lottie the story of the treasure inside.

"Your Grandad gave me this on the day your daddy graduated from high school," Gran said, opening the box and showing Lottie the ring inside. "One of his friends told him about a magical place in Florida, called Anna Maria Island, where the water was blue and the sand was white. My Brian gave me this ring as a promise that after your dad graduated from IU we would go there for a vacation and look for a little house where we could retire."

Gran handed Lottie the ring, and she stared at in in awe. The stone was a square-cut aquamarine, surrounded by channel set diamonds down the platinum band. Gran told her the aquamarine was to represent the aqua water of the Gulf of Mexico, and the diamonds represented the white sandy beach of Anna Maria Island. Lottie was certain she had never seen anything more beautiful in her life.

"As you know," Gran continued, the sadness coming back in her voice, "Brian was killed in a farming accident just a little over a year later, and we never made our trip to Anna Maria. I've often thought that's why your daddy went there that year on his spring break, so that he could see the beauty for himself. He either called me in the morning to tell me about the glory of the sunrise, or in the evening to tell me about the amazing sunset, but he never failed to call." Gran smiled again. "The one thing he didn't tell me was about the beautiful girl he had met."

Lottie looked at Gran and back at the ring and felt her own tears start to well-up. "You always seem so happy when you come to the island, Gran," Lottie said. "Doesn't it hurt to be there, knowing all that you lost?"

Gran brushed her fingertips gently over Lottie's tears and tipped her chin up so they could be eye to eye. "I did lose a lot, my sweet girl, but those losses brought me you, and for that I am ever grateful. That's why I want you to have this ring when the time is right. It was the last big gift I ever got from your grandad, and since it all ties back to Anna Maria Island, it should belong to you."

Lottie was at a loss for words, but not a loss for emotion as the tears continued to fall. She threw her arms around Gran's neck and they held each other tight for a few minutes. Lottie couldn't begin to imagine all the heartache her gran had faced, but she knew how blessed she was to have Gran in her life, and she wanted to do all she could to bring joy to her life.

"If I ever get married," Lottie told Gran, "I'd like this to be my engagement ring. That is if it's okay with you?"

"I can't think of anything I'd like more," Gran told her, "and I'll keep this ring safe and secure until that time comes. You haven't already picked out the young man, have you?" Gran teased, knowing how close Lottie and Nick were.

Lottie blushed a deep shade of red. "Gran!" she exclaimed. "I'm only sixteen, I've got a whole life ahead of me before I think about getting married!" But in her heart, Lottie hoped someday Nick would feel for her what she felt for him, and their friendship would turn into the forever kind of love Gran had with the grandfather she had never met.

Gran had ruffled her hair and said with a twinkle in her eye, "Of course not, Lottie, what was I thinking? Now how about we leave this stuffy old room and go get some lunch?"

Chapter 75

Now

"Charlotte? Charlotte, are you okay, you're scaring me?" she heard through the fog in her brain. Nick was still down on one knee, and the look on his face was as close to terrified as she had ever seen on him. By now, Maggie had moved around to Charlotte's side of the table and looked pretty worried herself.

Charlotte lifted her hand, stroked Nick's cheek, and started to smile. "Yes, Nick, yes!" she cried. "Of course, I'll marry you!" He engulfed her in his arms, and they both let the tears roll without any concern or embarrassment.

Everyone in the room stood and applauded, but before they could get to the happy couple to offer congratulations, Charlotte had to talk with her mom.

"So, tell me," Charlotte said to her mom right after Nick slid the ring on her finger, "how did Nick get Gran's ring, and how did you get involved? "

"Well," Maggie laughed, "I've been holding on to that ring since the day of your graduation from IU. Your gran gave it to me for safe keeping until, as she put it, you and Nick got your head out of your asses and realized you were meant to be together."

Charlotte blushed and covered her mouth to suppress a squeal. "Mom!" she exclaimed. "Gran said no such thing."

"Maybe not in those exact words," Maggie replied, "but that was her meaning. Anyway, I had the ring and when Nick called me right after the Fourth of July to ask for your hand, I told him about it, and we started making arrangements for me to get the ring to him. Of course, neither one of us knew there would be a few complications before he could propose."

Charlotte's heart was beating about a thousand beats per minute as she looked at Nick. "You called my mom after our weekend together, and you were going to ask me to marry you then?"

"I wish the whole mess with the Neels hadn't gotten in the way, but yes, I was going to ask you as soon as I got the ring. The plan was for your mom to send it to Pop, but once I knew the arrest for Tony was happening that week, I called Maggie and asked her to hold off. I expected you to be upset, but I underestimated your veracity about Carol. I'm just so happy we can finally move forward and start our future together. That night at your cottage I could feel my dream slipping away, and I've got to tell you, it was the worst night of my life."

"It was the worst night of mine, too," Charlotte told him softly, but the kiss that erupted was anything but soft.

The crowd wouldn't be contained any longer, and Becca made sure she was the first person to get to Charlotte. "So, surprises aren't always a bad thing, are they?" Becca laughed as she admired Charlotte's ring. "Do you have any idea how hard it was to be with you all week and not give anything away?"

Hugging her friend, Charlotte agreed that at least this surprise had a happy ending. As the rest of the guests made their way to Nick and Charlotte, she silently thanked her gran, and told her once more how much she loved her. Touching her locket, she smiled as she realized she would now have two constant reminders of her grandmother, and the special bond they had shared.

Chapter 76

Now

Maya gave the guests a few minutes to offer Nick and Charlotte their congratulations, and then she and Dimi brought out flutes filled with champagne for toasting. Nick refused one because he was still on medication, and Charlotte smiled and shook her head, seemingly in support of Nick. When Charlotte looked up and noticed a small grin on her mother's face, she looked away. *Shit, shit, shit! This is not good.*

Finally, the well-wishes came to an end and as people were milling around the room, talking and laughing, Maggie approached Charlotte and Nick. "Can I talk with you a minute, Lottie?" her mom asked.

"Alone?" Charlotte responded, a little afraid of what her mom had to say.

"I guess that's up to you," Maggie responded.

Worrying she might have something unkind to say about Nick, Charlotte took her Mom's arm and led her to a quiet corner. "So, what's going on? Charlotte asked, to gain control of the situation. "How did you get here, Mom?"

Maggie seemed a little miffed as she answered. "Well, I was wondering when you were going to share the news that I'm going to be a grandmother? And as to how I got here, I flew."

Charlotte could feel the color staining her cheeks as she replied. "You know about the baby?" she asked in confusion. "How?"

Finally, Maggie let go of her hurt and smiled. "I know you better than most of the people in this room, Charlotte Luce," she told her daughter. "I can see, even though your face is thinner, your hips have spread a little, and that's a dead give-a-way! Besides, you turned down champagne, and no one turns down champagne!"

"Seriously!" Charlotte exclaimed. "I don't know if I'm more upset because you think my hips have spread or because that one little thing is all it took for you to know I'm pregnant. Because, yes Mom, I am pregnant, and you're going to be a grandmother. Does that bother you?"

"Oh, Honey," Maggie said as she hugged her only child. "I'm thrilled I'm going to be a grandmother, and I can see how much you and Nick love each other, so the only thing that bothers me is that you didn't tell me sooner."

"I'm sorry Mom, I know I should have but I was afraid. I didn't want to let you down or make you feel…" Charlotte stopped what she was saying and looked at her mother.

"Like you were following in my footsteps?" Maggie answered quietly. "You're a grown woman Charlotte with a master's degree and so many achievements, I can't begin to name them all. I wish I had been more like you, but I fell in love and let my heart lead me. To be honest, we're not that much different, are we? You've always been in love with Nick, and you let your heart lead you back to him, and believe it or not, I really am happy for both of you."

Charlotte could see the love on her mom's face as they stood there together. "I hope I can be as understanding a mother as you are," Charlotte told her. "I'm sorry, Mom, I didn't tell you about the baby sooner, and I hope you'll want to be a part of its life. You and Thomas, that is. Where is my soon to be step-father?"

Maggie laughed. "He had a customer in Georgia who wanted to commission a sculpture, so we flew in to Tampa together, and I called an Uber to bring me here while he flew back to Atlanta. That means I'll be needing a place to stay for the weekend. I hope you still have an open guest room?"

It was all Charlotte could do to keep from groaning out loud, but instead she smiled and said, "Of course, Mom, you're welcome anytime." Now all she had to do was explain to Nick that the special night she'd offered him earlier was coming off the table.

Chapter 77

Now

It was after midnight when all the guests had said their goodbyes, and the only people remaining were family and the closest of friends. "So, tell me please," Charlotte addressed Nick's sister, "was a party for Nick all just a ploy to get me here unwittingly? It worked, that's for sure, but you went to an awful lot of trouble to help Nick surprise me."

Maya shook her head. "When I asked you and Nick last week about a party to honor him, that's exactly what I had in mind, but he called me while you were at the spa and coerced me into changing things up a bit. I hope you're not upset with me Lottie, I just wanted to make my brother happy."

Charlotte gave Maya a hug and grinned. "Everything about it was perfect Maya, and it's going to be a great story to tell Babycakes someday."

"Babycakes?" Maggie questioned. "Who in the world is Babycakes?"

"It's our grandchild, Margaret," Pop chimed in. "I guess we aren't going to know if it's a boy or a girl until it gets here."

Everyone laughed and Jared suggested they get on the road. "We're not used to these late nights," he admitted. "I'm pretty sure our kids will be up at the crack of dawn and ready to head for home."

Maggie told Charlotte that she was going to ride with Noah, Pop, and Shelly and not to expect her for a while since they had to drop Shelly off at her house in Tampa. Charlotte was trying not to make eye contact with Nick, but he found a way to get her attention and raised his eyebrows, as if to question her mother's remark.

Doing her best to ignore him, Charlotte made her way around the room giving hugs and her thanks for a wonderful evening, before she walked out of the restaurant with Nick and the Tylers. Nick walked her around to her side of the car and made sure she was safely buckled in, but after he fastened his own seatbelt, he looked at her, and she saw the frustration on his face.

"Your mother is staying at your house with you?" Nick questioned in his controlled FBI voice. "I guess that means that I'm not?" Nick got that Charlotte wasn't comfortable sleeping with him when someone else was around, but dammit, he had waited patiently for her these past few weeks, and this night should be theirs!

"What else could I do, Nick? She flew in today to be here for us, and her things are at Maya's. I couldn't very well try to get Maya to keep her, and it's a little late to be looking for a motel." Charlotte looked so miserable that Nick couldn't stay upset with her. He held her hand and tried to take the high road.

"I was really looking forward to tonight," he told her huskily. "I guess it's a good thing blue's my favorite color. I've watched you prance around in that dress all night, and I can tell I'm going to pay for the thoughts I've been having."

Jared started to laugh while Charlotte sat there trying to understand what he was saying, when suddenly it hit her. "Nick!" she cried, slapping him softly on the arm. "I can't believe you just said that in front of our friends."

"A guy's got to get pleasure wherever he can," he said, smiling at her. "Although this pleasure is nothing compared to what I had in mind."

Becca and Jared looked at each other, knowing when they got back to her parent's house, they wouldn't be confined to any boundaries, and Charlotte just groaned. She knew all about the kind of pleasure Nick Greyson could provide, and those thoughts had been swirling around in her mind all night, too.

Chapter 78

Now

By the time the foursome arrived back in AMI both Charlotte and Becca were sound asleep. Charlotte had a crick in her neck from trying to lay her head on Nick's shoulder while buckled in a seatbelt, and she could barely get her eyes opened when he tried to wake her up.

"What is it about dinners at Stavros that put me to sleep?" Charlotte said as she exited the car. "Do you think everything is secretly made with turkey?"

Nick shrugged his shoulders as if to say, "I have no clue," and then escorted her up the walk. With Charlotte's house keys in his hand, Nick helped her inside the little cottage on the beach. "I really am sorry about tonight, Nick," she said between yawns. "It means a lot that you understand I just couldn't make love with you while my mother is in the next room."

Nick pulled her close and started kissing and nuzzling her neck. When he got to her ear he whispered, "Oh Baby, making love is not at all what I had planned for tonight, but we would have gotten around to it eventually."

Charlotte's whole body reacted as she remembered the amazing things Nick had done the first time they had been together, as well as the soft and sensual ones later in the weekend. "You're not playing fair," she pouted.

And he replied, "I know." Giving her forehead a gentle kiss, Nick moved towards the door. "I don't want to leave you, but if you're not going to let me stay, I need to let Becca and Jared get home." With a grin he added, "This will be the first time I've kissed my fiancé goodnight so I want to make it memorable."

And boy did he! Charlotte was trembling when he finally pulled away, and it was all she could do not to beg him to stay. "I love you, Charlotte," Nick said seriously. "I can't wait to start our life together." With one more kiss, this one with a little less passion, Nick walked out.

Charlotte was exhausted, but her mind and body were on full alert. Kicking off her beautiful new Manalos, she reached around to unfasten her party dress. She had loved the way it looked, and the airy material had been perfect for a hot summer's night event. She carefully hung it up so it didn't wrinkle.

Turning around she saw herself in the full-length mirror on the back of the closet and sighed. She was standing there in nothing but the pair of sheer, black silk, French-cut panties she had purchased especially for this night, and Nick hadn't even known! What is it about me wearing black lingerie that never turns out the way I imagine? Charlotte asked herself. Throwing the tiny wisp of material in the hamper she decided from now on she'd stick with pastels.

Before moving away from the mirror, Charlotte ran her hand over her enlarging tummy and talked with her unborn child. "Your daddy and I are going to get married, Babycakes. I would have taken good care of you on my own, I want you to know that. We're going to be a family, and it's what you deserve. It's what we all deserve, and I promise you'll never feel alone or unloved. Not ever."

Turning around so she could get a look at her backside she added, "And your Grandma's wrong! My hips have definitely not spread!"

Throwing on her IU nightshirt, Charlotte grabbed her cell phone and crawled into bed to wait for her mom to call and say she needed to be let in the house. Had she told her she would call? No, but Charlotte knew she wouldn't be able to get inside without her help, so sleep would have to wait. She lifted-up her left hand and wiggled her ring finger so the gorgeous new engagement ring adorning it could catch the moonlight. "I'm the luckiest girl in the world," she sighed, and then, just like she knew it would, her cell phone rang. Seeing her mom's name in the caller ID, Charlotte didn't bother to answer but headed straight to the front door.

Chapter 79

Now

"Hi Honey," Maggie said sheepishly. "I forgot to ask you to leave a key outside for me." Maggie walked into the room, carrying a large suitcase and gave her daughter a once-over.

"That sleep shirt is older than dirt, Lottie," Maggie scolded. "Surely Nick deserves something a little sexier, especially tonight of all nights."

Charlotte was not in the mood to have this conversation with her mother. "Nick isn't here, Mom," she said with a little more force than Maggie was used to.

"What do you mean, he isn't here? I naturally assumed you two were living together."

Charlotte sighed and tried to stay firm, yet respectful. "We're not living together, Mom, but he would have come home with me if the circumstances were different." Letting out a big breath she continued. "Since I'm pregnant, it's obvious that we've slept together, but we like to keep our private life private. Anyway, I do, so while you're here, he won't be making any overnight visits."

"I didn't mean to cause a problem, Lottie," her mom told her. "I guess we're not as much alike as I thought. If that hunk belonged to me, I wouldn't let him out of my sight."

"Let me take you to your room, Mom," Charlotte said with a little frustration," and from now on, will you please call me Charlotte? I'm not your little girl anymore."

Maggie smiled and followed Charlotte down the hall. "You've definitely gotten a backbone these last few years," Maggie said with a smirk. "I think I like it. Charlotte."

Charlotte couldn't help but laugh as she said, "I love you too, Mom, and now I need some sleep. There are fresh towels in the guest bathroom, and the Keurig and some pods are on the counter in the kitchen. Juice and fruit are in the fridge if you get up and I'm gone, and there are usually bagels in the freezer. Feel free to help yourself to anything, that is except my boyfriend, no my fiancé. You may be my mom, but you're still a gorgeous woman, and that hunk is all mine."

Feeling pretty proud of herself, Charlotte headed to her room for some much-needed sleep. Just as she was getting comfortable, her cell pinged and she read the text. "I miss you, I need you, and I love you. Goodnight beautiful."

Charlotte snuggled down into her bed and let her mind lead her to sweet and spicy dreams!

Chapter 80

Now

Unable to sleep much past six, Charlotte finally got up and decided she needed to run. Sending Nick a text that read, "Good Morning! Are you up for a run?" she grabbed a pair of shorts and a sports bra and headed to the bathroom.

She didn't even have her hair up before Nick replied. "Stayed up late with Noah but give me ten and I'll be ready. Coffee for the ride?"

Charlotte finished dressing, gave her face a quick wash, brushed her teeth, and headed to the kitchen to make Nick a to-go cup of coffee. She hadn't had any signs of morning sickness for a while but decided to fix herself a glass of juice to go instead.

She wrote a quick note to her mom, letting her know where she was going, and smiled as she realized maybe she was still her mother's little girl after all. *Old habits die hard*, she thought, sticking her keys and phone in her pocket and grabbing the two drinks.

Even this early in the morning, with only a few hours' sleep, Nick looked like an underwear model as he waited for her outside the marina. He hadn't shaved, and his jaw was covered with a sexy dark stubble. His hair was messy and curling a little bit over his forehead.

"Hey," Charlotte said as she looked him up and down. "Maybe we should get our exercise another way."

Nick groaned. "I love this little car of yours, but it's nowhere near big enough for me to lay down in, and I know neither my room nor yours is nearly private enough for you."

"Who said anything about lying down?" Charlotte teased him. "Oh well, I guess you missed your chance!"

"You'll pay for that Miss Luce," Nick replied, but he got into the car and took his coffee, without much fuss.

"So," Charlotte began, "it's the weekend, and you said you had some things to tell me over the weekend. So, spill it, big guy."

"Are you freakin' kidding me?" Nick asked. "You got me up at the crack of dawn, saying you wanted to run, when all you really wanted was to find out what I said I had to talk with you about? Pretty sneaky, Charlotte."

She tried to act embarrassed, but just couldn't pull it off. "I guess all those years of reading mysteries paid off," she giggled. "Maybe I should have talked with Director James about working for the FBI?"

"The FBI is one of the things we need to discuss, but I really need this coffee first." Nick took a big swig, leaving Charlotte to stew over what it was he had to say. Was he close to going back to work? Did they have another big case for him? Her mind was going a million miles an hour.

By the time Nick finished his coffee, Charlotte was pulling into the parking area of the Botanical Gardens and about to blow her top. "Nicholas Michael Greyson, if you don't tell me this minute what's going on I'll—"

"You'll do what, Sis?" he retorted.

Realizing she did sound just like Maya in her Mama Bear mode, Charlotte took a breath and calmed down. "I'm sorry, Nick," she told him. "I didn't mean to sound like a shrew, it's just your job scares me, but I know it's something I'm going to have to learn to deal with."

"I won't tell Maya you compared her to a shrew," he laughed, "but between us, she can be one from time to time. You may like my news if you have concerns about my job."

It was all Charlotte could do not to resort to pleading as Nick sat there with a grin on his face, but somehow, she did it. After about a minute, that felt like an hour, Nick began to talk.

"So," he asked her seriously, "how would you feel if I didn't go back to the FBI?"

Chapter 81

Now

"What are you saying, Nick?" Charlotte implored. "You love your job, why wouldn't you be going back?"

"I've told you before how I ended up with the FBI, and yes, I did enjoy it, but it was never my dream. Coach Donavan came to see me this week, Charlotte, and he's ready to retire and asked me to consider taking over for him. I have an opportunity now to make all of my dreams come true."

The way Nick was looking in her eyes was all it took for Charlotte to lose control. She threw herself in his arms and started to bawl. "Oh Nick, if only you knew." She spat out between sobs.

"So, are those happy tears?" he asked tentatively.

"The happiest," she said, trying to get herself back under control. "I've not been able to get the picture of you strapped down on that hospital bed out of my mind, and it's not something I ever wanted either one of us to go through again."

Stroking her back, Nick's response was gentle. "That makes two of us, Charlotte. But if you hated my job so much, why didn't you say something?"

"Because it wasn't my place to. Being in love with you didn't give me the right to try to change your life, Nick," she told him as she wiped away the last of the tears. "Having you make the decision is the answer to prayer."

"How about instead of a run we walk down to the koi pond and find a bench?" Nick asked her. "There are still some things we need to discuss before I make a job change, plus I have a question to ask you."

"I already agreed to marry you," Charlotte said, lifting up her engagement ring for proof. "What else could you possibly want to ask me?"

"Let's take a walk," Nick answered, taking her hand in his, "and I'll tell you everything."

Chapter 82

Now

"I want to take you to meet my mom," Nick blurted out the minute they sat down.

Charlotte just sat there looking at him as if he were an alien. "Why?" she finally asked with a little sarcasm. "She couldn't even be bothered to come to the hospital after you were shot, and now you think she deserves a visit? I wonder what your dad would think of that."

"She's sick, Charlotte," was all Nick said, but the look on his face told her all she needed to know.

"I'm so sorry, Nick," Charlotte tried to soothe him. "What's wrong with her?"

"She has an autoimmune disease called Scleroderma, and to be honest, I'm really scared. Mom called me one day last week while you were with Becca, and we've been talking every day since. I don't condone the way she shipped us back to Pop, pretending that Hudson wanted to travel, and we were in the way, but at least I understand it now. Regardless of the past, she's my mom, and I love her."

Charlotte had never seen Nick so emotional, and it was really frightening. "If you want me to meet your mother, you know I will, but it would help if I knew more. I can see how upset you are, and it's breaking my heart."

Letting out the huge breath he'd been holding in, Nick started to speak. "I found out a lot through the phone calls we've been having, and after I tell you Mom's story, I need to tell my family. I know I should have probably talked with them first, but I really need your support with this. I meant what I said last night, Charlotte, you've always been the one person to make me feel complete, and I need you to help me get my family through this."

Charlotte brushed a lock of hair from Nick's forehead and gently stroked his cheek. "I'm here for you Nick, no matter what you need," she told him gently. "That's what love is all about, isn't it? That's what my Gran had with my Grandad, and it's what I want for us."

Nick nodded and bent down with a kiss. It wasn't a hot and passionate kiss like he usually gave her, but there was something about this kiss that meant so much more. For Charlotte, it said you're important to me and this is for real, and there was nothing to her that mattered more.

Taking Nick's hand Charlotte said, "How about we take a walk around these beautiful gardens, and you can tell me everything you've found out about your mom, okay?"

An hour later, they were back at the parking lot, and Charlotte's head was swimming. She realized now she had preconceived ideas about Nick's mom, and even though it pained her to say it, she knew now Pop was every bit as guilty in the break-up of their family as she had been.

She stood by her car, looking over the tranquil gardens, and rehashed in her head what Nick had just shared with her. After a big fight over how much her husband was working and how alone she felt with three young kids and no family close by, Elizabeth Greyson had fled, taking her children back to her hometown, running away from the man she loved and his life on Anna Maria Island. She thought for sure he would come after them, and he thought for sure she would cool off and come home. Instead, they both held on to their anger and pride, and the family was shattered. The story was so similar to what had happened between them, that Charlotte wanted nothing more than to grab Nick and hold on tight.

"So, your mom found out she had scleroderma shortly after the divorce was final and married an old boyfriend because he promised to take care of all of you? That's just so sad."

"I think Hudson loved Mom and wanted everything to work out, but as soon as the disease started to show on her physically, they both

210

knew we kids would be better off with Pop. Once again, our mother let pride get in her way. That's why she made up the story about not being able to travel with three children in tow."

"Hudson died about five years later," Nick continued, "and Mom married Gus almost right away. For about a decade she was in remission, but once the disease came back, it came back with a vengeance. It's obvious Mom is still in love with Pop, but she refuses to let him see her the way she is. Gus has taken great care of her, and I appreciate that, but I feel really sorry for the guy. His wife is terminally ill, and he knows she's always been in love with another man. It's the epitome of hell, if you ask me."

Charlotte wrapped herself around him and laid her head on Nick's shoulder. "That could be us, Nick," she told him. "We could have wasted our whole lives refusing to forgive and forget, and I hate that I was the one who held on to the hurt and the anger. Can you ever forgive me?"

Nick smiled for the first time since he started telling her about his parents. "We both made mistakes, Charlotte, but we found ourselves back where we belong, and it's all that matters. So, I'm asking you again, will you go with me to see my mom? I really want you to meet her before she gets any worse."

"Yes, Nick," Charlotte said with a grin. "I'd love to go meet the woman who brought the love of my life into this world."

"Great," he said with a smile, "because we're leaving on Monday!"

Chapter 83

Now

"What do you mean we're leaving on Monday?" Charlotte demanded. "That's only two days away, and besides, I just now agreed to go."

"I guess I was counting on my devilishly good looks to help you see things my way," Nick said with a chuckle. "The thing is, I was pretty confident on you being okay with my job change, too, so I kind of told Coach Donavan I would accept his offer." Nick stopped for a moment to gage Charlotte's reaction before continuing, "and, taking the job, means going back to school, and it starts the following Wednesday. That's why we need to go to New York now."

Charlotte was fuming but tried to hold her temper. "I see," she said coldly. "While I am thrilled to think of you leaving the FBI, and I do want to meet your mother, I don't like being railroaded, Nick, and that's exactly how this feels. I'm not used to having my life arranged for me, and that can't change, regardless of our relationship."

"I get that, Charlotte," Nick said contritely. "I promise I'll do better, but everything happened so fast and with Becca here we just didn't have a good time to talk. I can cancel the reservations if you want me to, but if I'm going to take over for the Coach next semester, I have to get my teaching accreditation now. My Criminal Justice degree is a big help, but I need more sociology and civics credits if I'm going to teach. But I don't want you to be unhappy, so this is your call."

Charlotte looked up at his handsome face, and yes, it was a devilishly handsome one, and she sighed. "Okay, Nick, we'll leave on Monday for New York, because I really want you to take that job at the high school. But just so we're clear, from now on, we discuss things that affect us as a couple before making decisions. Agreed?"

"Agreed," he told her. "Definitely, agreed."

They were both quiet for the first few minutes of the ride and then Charlotte spoke up. "Should we be discussing our finances?" she asked.

"Always the accountant, aren't you?" Nick responded. "But you don't need to worry, Charlotte, because even though this teaching job won't be as lucrative as the one with the FBI, I'll still be able to take care of you and Babycakes."

"You're such a guy!" she laughed.

"I thought that was one of the things you liked about me," Nick smirked.

"Oh, it is, Nick, it is, but I don't need a man to take care of me. Maybe I should have told you this before, but when I graduated from IU my gran deeded the beach cottage over to me. I've lived there mortgage free all these years, but that's not all. She also gave me the rent money she'd collected on the house for over twenty years. What I'm saying is, I invested that money well so neither one of us would have to work again if we didn't want to."

Charlotte stopped talking long enough to let her revelation sink in, and said to Nick, "Say something."

Placing his hand gently on her tummy, Nick addressed their unborn child. "It sounds to me like we've got us a Sugar Mama, Babycakes. Not only is she a mogul, but she's beautiful, too."

"So, you're okay with everything?" Charlotte asked him. "I mean, I do still owe Owen Gardner for Carol's defense, but since her charges were dropped, it shouldn't be much."

"By okay, do you mean does it bother me to think about being a kept man? Hell no, but while I'm not exactly on your level moneywise, my Jeep and condo are both paid for, and if we're going to live on the island, I can sell the condo and have a nice nest egg. We are going to live on the island, right? That's a big reason I wanted the teaching job."

"I do want to stay in Anna Maria, and I was hoping you would, too." Charlotte told him. "I was also hoping that after we get married, you would be okay living in my beach house? It's the last real connection to Gran I have, besides my locket and ring, that is, and I love them so much."

"Home for me is wherever you are, and if the cottage is where you want to be, it's where I want to be," Nick answered. Taking her hand, he added, "Now that we have all that out of the way, maybe it's time to talk about what really matters, and that's our wedding."

Chapter 84

Now

They pulled-up to the marina parking lot and Charlotte put her head on the steering wheel. "You've given me more than enough to think about for one day," she told him with a groan. "My brain is on overload as it is, so wedding talk is going to be put on hold."

"I thought her wedding was something a girl planned for her whole life," Nick answered. "I want you to have whatever you want, but one thing I won't compromise on is our being married before Babycakes makes its appearance."

Charlotte saw the stern look on his face, and she loved his chivalry, but unlike most girls, planning her wedding had never been a large part of her thought process. "I want us to be married before the baby is born too, Nick. Since we just became engaged last night, I haven't really had time to think about anything, let alone a wedding. Can we please make it through this weekend with my mom, go to New York to see your mom, and when we get home, we talk about a wedding? We still have plenty of time before my due date."

"I guess I don't have a choice," Nick grumbled. "I know you need to get home to your mom, so call me later when we can get back together. I want to talk with Pop and Noah about Mom either tonight or tomorrow, and I have to call Maya before we leave on Monday."

Charlotte could see the dark clouds in Nick's eyes, and she knew he was hurt that she wasn't ready to discuss getting married, but she couldn't back down. They still had a lot to learn about each other, and she realized it was starting now.

"I'll call you after I find out more about Mom's plans," she told him, and she drove away.

Charlotte unlocked the door to her cottage and heard first thing the sounds of passion coming from her guestroom. Her mother had been pretty free with her ideas about sex when Charlotte was growing-up, but now that she was engaged to Thomas, surely she wasn't entertaining another man? And in Charlotte's house!

"Mom?" Charlotte called out loudly so there was no confusion that she was home. Instead of her mother with an Oops! look on her face, a man came out of the room, shirtless, trying quickly to fasten his jeans.

"Lottie," the man said, stepping towards her, "I'm Thomas, your Mom's fiancé."

Charlotte looked at the man standing before her, trying to come up with something to say. He was about her height with imposing muscles and a shaved head. Charlotte gauged him to be about fifty and decided he looked more like a biker than an artist.

Just as Charlotte was about to open her mouth, her mom came rushing out of the bedroom, barely wrapped in a satin robe, her caramel colored hair sticking out all over her head. "Thomas flew into Tampa and drove here in a rental car, because he missed me so much! Wasn't that a wonderful surprise?"

Charlotte had experienced enough surprises for one day, but she didn't want to be rude to the man who had finally taken her mom's heart, so she smiled and said, "Wonderful."

Remembering she was still in her running clothes, Charlotte suggested that she shower and dress, and later the three of them could sit down and talk. Seeing that dreamy look in her mom's eyes, she was pretty sure she and Thomas would be heading back to bed while she got ready, but Charlotte didn't care, as long as there was no moaning coming through the walls. It didn't matter how old a girl was, hearing her mother having sex was just gross!

Chapter 85

Now

After a long, hot shower, Charlotte slipped into a pair of elastic waist Capri's, and a striped sleeveless blouse that was cute and loose enough to hide her growing belly. Pulling her hair into a high ponytail, she swiped her mouth with coconut lip gloss, and headed out of her room to officially meet Thomas Nelson.

Charlotte found her mom and Thomas sitting in the lanai, both properly dressed and behaving like parents. She saw the love they had for each other in their faces, and she mellowed a little, knowing her mom had finally found lasting happiness.

Thomas stood up when she walked in the room and put out his arms for a hug. "I'm glad to finally meet you, Lottie," he said as they embraced. "Your mom talks about you all the time, and she's right, you sure are a looker."

Thankful he couldn't see the blush creeping over her face, Charlotte responded. "I'm happy to meet you too, Thomas," she told him, "but will you please call me Charlotte? I'm trying to get Mom to see me as an adult and that means Lottie needs to go." Thomas nodded and stepped away from her, and Charlotte saw for the first time he was just what her mom needed.

After a long talk, Maggie told Charlotte she wanted to show Thomas around the island and take him to the Cortez Kitchen for lunch. She also told her they would be leaving on Monday to go back to Arizona, where the "Kitty" was being taken care of by friends. In all the excitement, Charlotte had forgotten to ask about her friend Carol. She was relieved to find out she was happy and flourishing in the artist colony where Maggie and Thomas lived.

Instead of calling Nick, Charlotte decided to drive to the marina and surprise him. Maybe it would help her get over her discomfort at surprises if she saw other people enjoying them. When she pulled-up to the marina and saw Nick, Pop, and Noah sitting on the deck with all three of them looking excited to see her, she decided surprises weren't so bad. Especially when she was the one doing the surprising!

Nick was really nervous when he started to tell his dad and brother about his recent conversations with his mom, but surprisingly it all went well. Charlotte held his hand and kept her eyes on him as he spoke, and she was very thankful both Pop and Noah seemed receptive to she and Nick going to New York for a visit.

"I loved Elizabeth for over half of my life," Pop began. "It breaks my heart that we let our own stupidity get in the way of our family, but I've finally let go of that love, and now I can only wish she's happy and isn't suffering." Charlotte saw the tears in Pop's eyes, and she wanted to comfort him, but she knew that this was something he needed to work through on his own. She was curious though as to whether her friend Shelly had anything to do with his letting go of his feelings for his ex-wife.

Noah slapped Nick on the back and thanked him for finding out the truth from their mom. "I always thought it was having me that put Mom over the edge," Noah admitted, "so maybe now, I can let go of the guilt."

Nick and Pop shared some stories of the good times they had as a family with Noah, who had been too young to remember, and all three decided harboring resentment at this point was futile. Pop's Lizzy, and Nick and Noah's Mom, needed their support now, and they all vowed to give it.

"Let's call Maya tonight after the girls go to bed," Pop said, "and we can tell her as a family. She was devastated when Elizabeth sent you kids home. Hopefully now, she can understand and accept why."

After more reminiscing, they decided to head to the Cortez Kitchen for lunch, in hopes that Nick could meet his prospective father-in-law, and where they could all enjoy a grouper sandwich and onion rings.

There just wasn't a much better way to spend a Saturday afternoon on AMI!

Chapter 86

Now

The rest of the weekend went well. Maya handled the news about her mother with a lot of tears but a lot of compassion. Charlotte was amazed at how forgiving and loving the three Greyson children were and vowed she would also put her judgment of Elizabeth Greyson behind her, accepting Nick's mom as they had.

As it turned out, Maggie and Thomas were flying out of Tampa International Airport within an hour of their flight into JFK, and Nick and Charlotte were able to hitch a ride with them, rather than leave a car at the airport. Pop and Noah agreed one of them would pick them up when they returned, so everything was working out great.

The time in the car gave Charlotte and Thomas an opportunity to get to know each other better, and by the time they reached the airport, they all felt like old friends. "I'm happy that we had these past two days together, Mom," Charlotte said, "and I really like Thomas." With a smile and a hug, she added, "he's perfect for you, and Nick and I are looking forward to coming out for your wedding."

Maggie hugged her daughter and replied, "We could make it a double wedding you know, it's only about another six weeks away."

Charlotte knew Nick wouldn't be put off that long, so she just responded, "We'll see."

The foursome parted company to head for their prospective airlines' waiting areas. When the time came for them to board, Charlotte grabbed Nick's hand and shared with him her discomfort of flying. "You can't let go until we touch down in New York, Nick, promise me you won't let go."

"I'm not ever letting go," he told her with a kiss to her hand, and together they walked down the tarmac. Just as they were ready to step onto the plane Charlotte kissed the first two fingers of her right hand and placed them on the airline logo. "Arrive alive," she said, and slipped into the plane.

"It's a good thing we don't have any carry-ons," Nick laughed, as he tried to sit down without letting go of Charlotte's hand. "I'm not sure how we would have gotten them into the overhead bins."

Charlotte smiled sweetly and realized they needed both hands to fasten their seatbelts, so she let go, but the minute they were snapped in place, Nick reached for her hand and held it securely in his lap.

By the time the plane touched down, Charlotte had relaxed and was ready for an adventure in New York City. Her clients back on the island were taken care of for the week, her Mom was in love with a terrific guy, and she was finally going to meet Nick's mom!

Nick told her he would get the luggage while Charlotte made a trip to the lady's room and they would meet by the red exit sign. She had just found her way there when she heard her name being called. By two different voices.

"Charlotte?" she heard the voice from her past ask, while at the same time she heard Nick calling, "Charlotte?" Looking up she stared into the exotic lavender grey eyes of the man whose heart she had taken, to the beautiful blue ones of the man she had given her heart to.

Standing there, confronted by the two special men whom she genuinely cared about, all she could think of were the three little words she had said to them both.

Shit! Shit! Shit!

To be continued in Book Three, *The Greysons*
Turn the page for a preview.

Preview

The Greysons

Nick helped me into the backseat of the cab without uttering a word. Once he was seated and buckled in, he gave the driver the go ahead, and we were on our way to his mother and step-father's Park Avenue apartment. Before we left the airport, I could see his eyes had turned stormy and dark, a sure sign he was hurting but trying to hide it. I reached over and took his hand, and thankfully he didn't pull away, but his face was still turned towards the window.

"Nick," I said softly, "please look at me." I waited a moment for him to respond before gently rubbing my thumb over his fingers. He didn't look at me, but he did squeeze my hand, and the little gesture helped me to breathe again, at least for the moment.

"My name is Charlotte Luce, and just four days ago the beautiful man sitting next to me, the one with his nose almost pressed against the glass, asked me to marry him. This whole summer has been one drama after another, but I really thought it was all behind us now and Nick and I could finally be happy. Did I mention that I'm pregnant? That's just one part of the drama I fondly call, The Nick and Charlotte Show."

Nick finally turned his head and looked at me and I saw the hurt and regret written all over his face. I thought my heart would break then, but it really shattered when he started to speak.

"He's still in love with you, you know," Nick said quietly.

I grabbed my locket and said another silent prayer to Gran. The way this day was going, I was definitely in need of her help!

Scheduled for release in 2019

About The Author

I hope that you enjoyed Call Me Charlotte, and I invite you to leave a review on Amazon and/or Goodreads. It's only through feedback that I can become the best author I can be, and it also helps others to know what books they want to read.

Please visit me at DanaLBrownBooks.com for information and upcoming events.

- Join my author page on Facebook @DanaLBrownAuthor
- And Twitter @DanaLBrownBook

Wishing you a Happy Ending!
Dana L

Discussion Questions

1. What was your initial reaction to the book? Did it hook you immediately, or take some time to get into?

2. Do you think the story was plot-based or character driven?

3. What was your favorite quote/passage?

4. What made the setting unique or important? Could the story have taken place anywhere?

5. Did you pick out any themes throughout the book?

6. How did the characters change throughout the story? How did your opinion of them change?

7. Which character did you relate to the most, and what was it about them that you connected with?

8. How did you feel about the ending? What did you like, what did you not like, and what do you wish had been different?

9. If the book were being adapted into a movie, who would you want to see play what parts?

10. How did the structure of the book affect the story?